Hiding in
Hawk's Creek

Hiding in
Hawk's Creek

Brenda Chapman

Napoleon

Toronto, Ontario, Canada

Cover art by Patty Gallinger

Published by Napoleon Publishing
Toronto, Ontario, Canada

Le Conseil des Arts
du Canada | The Canada Council
for the Arts

Napoleon Publishing acknowledges the support of the Canada Council for our publishing program.

Printed in Canada

10 09 08 07 06   5 4 3 2 1

Library and Archives Canada Cataloguing in Publication

Chapman, Brenda, date-
        Hiding in Hawk's Creek / Brenda Chapman.

ISBN 1-894917-24-3

        I. Title.
PS8605.H36H53 2006   jC813'.6   C2006-900039-5

For Donna Russell and
Steve Chapman
and our northern childhood

One

My mother said that she wouldn't be a teenager again for all the tea in China. I think I agree with her for once, because my life starting resembling the *Titanic* about the time I entered high school. With grades that had slipped from average to barely passing, a completely dysfunctional family, and a long, boring vacation ahead of me, I was not looking forward to my fourteenth summer in Springhills. In fact, I was counting the days until I could be on my own, away from Mom and Mr. Putterman, away from Dad and Uncle Phil and far, far away from Morton T. High and everybody in it.

Okay, maybe I was exaggerating *just* a little. I'd miss Ambie, my best friend since kindergarten, and Leslie, my little sister, who had her own plans this summer. I'd even miss Pete Flaghert, in spite of the promise I'd made to myself to forget about him. He'd been going out with Angela Frost all through high school and treating me like the sister he'd always wanted. It didn't take a crystal ball to tell me where that was leading.

During the last days of the school term, I'd told myself that I was just waiting for the right moment to tell Mom that I was planning to spend the summer in Hawk's Creek with Grandma Connelly. I'd convinced myself that what Mom'd mind most was losing a babysitter for Leslie, because it seemed like I'd spent the last two years of my life rushing home so that Leslie wouldn't be left alone while Mom worked crazy nursing shifts at the hospital. I didn't like to think that part of me was scared to leave Springhills because everything was changing so fast. Already there was a distance between Mom and me that I couldn't explain. Dad had become moody, and Leslie was hanging out more and more with her own friends. My world was spinning out of control, and I needed to spend a summer up north, where I could be by myself, becoming one with the birch trees and the moose.

My best opportunity to approach Mom about going away for the month of July came one Friday evening after we'd eaten the spaghetti dinner I'd cooked while Mom was at work. She'd come home late from Springhills Hospital, and before sitting down to eat, she'd kicked off her shoes and poured herself a glass of red wine. She was still wearing her white nurse's uniform, and before eating, tucked a paper towel under her chin to catch the tomato splatter. She was in a pretty good mood and talked non-stop while she twirled slightly overcooked spaghetti on her fork.

"Jen, that was wonderful," she finally said, pushing her plate away and patting her tummy. She smiled at me and stretched her arms to the ceiling. "You're turning into a wonderful cook." My mom's face beams like sunshine when she's happy. I knew my cooking wasn't going to win any awards, but it was nice that Mom always ate it without complaint. I didn't mind taking compliments either.

"Thanks, Mom. Stay sitting. We'll clean up." I wanted her good mood to last.

While Leslie and I were doing the dishes, I kept glancing at Mom, trying to make certain nothing was upsetting her, while she flipped through the newspaper at the kitchen table. I'd learned that her good humour could disappear faster than my allowance. She'd told me a few months back that with everything going on, she might want Leslie and me to stick around home for the summer. I was hoping she'd forgotten. Finally, I took the plunge and asked, "Mom, do you think it would be okay if I visited Grandma Connelly in July?" I held my breath.

Mom raised her head and took off her reading glasses. "Well...I was hoping you'd find a job in Springhills for the summer. You know, I saw a sign in Pago's yesterday. They're looking for a salesgirl to work evenings and weekends."

Great. I could spend my summer selling clothes to my friends. I was going to have to think fast, or the holiday would be a complete write-off. "I think they've already found somebody." I crossed my fingers, praying the fib wouldn't come back to bite me. "And besides, I'd really like to visit Grandma for a few weeks. I think she could use some help around her place. At least, it looked that way when we visited last summer."

Mom tapped the arm of her glasses against her teeth. "Hmmm. I guess a few weeks at Grandma's would be okay." She looked at Leslie, who had stopped drying the plate that she'd been rubbing with a plaid tea towel. "What about you, honey? Do you want to go to Grandma's too?"

Leslie shook her head. "Molly and I are going to ballerina camp. They have the beginner camp only in July. *Remember?*" Molly and Leslie had dreamed of being ballerinas ever since Dad took them to see *Swan Lake* in Toronto. Leslie's expressive brown eyes, the mirror images of Dad's, flashed accusingly at Mom.

Mom tapped her forehead. "Of course. I forgot for a minute." Her eyes rested on me. "Maybe you could wait until August this year, Jennifer."

I didn't want to wait. I played my trump card. "Dad wants me to work in his garage this summer. I guess I could just do that."

It tipped the scales as I knew it would. Mom answered quickly. "There's no need for you to be dragged down with his latest ill thought-out project. I guess we can manage for a few weeks in July." Then she sighed. "Why can't he just take a job working for someone else and not

4

risk putting himself in the poorhouse?" She pursed her lips together and got a set look on her face, like ping-pong balls could bounce off her cheeks.

I knew Leslie was trying not to look at me, and I could tell by the way she lowered her head that she was upset. For over two years, she'd kept the flame alive, believing that Mom and Dad were going to work things out. I was always amazed at how she could pretend bad things weren't really happening. I, on the other hand, had quickly figured out that the truce my parents had reached after Dad returned to Springhills was going to be shorter-lived than the cherry red miniskirts stretched across the mannequins in Pago's store window. This cloud was not one with a silver lining.

*   *   *

That memorable June afternoon, the day all hope for Bannon happiness went down the toilet, the three of us had been sitting around the kitchen table drinking lemonade. Leslie was dressed in the Snoopy costume that she'd worn for Hallowe'en, waiting for her best friend Molly to come over and play "dogs". I probably didn't mention that Leslie is ten and a half and has so far resisted the lure of teenagehood. It was my final day of Grade Nine, and one of those hot June days that blows in like a breath of the summer that is to come. I remember feeling that day like the concrete slab I'd been carrying around on my head had just slid off. Miraculously, I'd passed all my school subjects, even though it hadn't looked very promising before Christmas break, when Mom had been asked by the school to find me a tutor. I'd managed to talk my way out of that idea, but it had meant spending way more time studying than I would have liked in order to keep Mom from pulling me off the school basketball team. Sometimes, a compromise doesn't always work in your favour; I'd pretty much had no social life for the entire last semester. What was even more amazing was that I hadn't realized how stressed I'd been until I'd read my final report card. I'd celebrated by eating half a carton of ice cream and a large pizza.

I looked over at Mom, who was fiddling with the lemonade jug, tracing the beads of moisture up and down the outside of the glass. Suddenly, she leaned across the table and tapped her finger on its wooden surface like she was making a point. "Girls, I'm going to marry John Putterman."

Right then, I understood what it means when they say that words hang in the air. Leslie and I sat as still as church mice, trying to take in the meaning of what she'd just thrown at us. I kept going over and over in my mind, "Mr. Putterman's going to marry Mom. Mr. Putterman's going to be my step-dad." I glanced over at Leslie. Her face had begun to crumple like she was going to cry. I talked fast. "Good news, Mom. I guess that will be good for you. Mr. Putterman is a good man. Maybe Leslie and I should throw you a party or something," I finished weakly. A party was the last thing we should throw them. And was "good" the only adjective I could come up with? My babbling seemed to work.

Mom beamed at me, "Oh, darling. A party is a nice idea, but John and I don't want any fuss." She leaned her head to one side and looked dreamily over our heads. "We actually were engaged last year, but we didn't want to talk about it, with everything going on."

I groaned inside. Talk about pouring salt into our open wound.

Engaged for a year—and we'd been dreaming all this time that Mom and Dad would get back together. "Everything going on" was Dad leaving town for two years without saying goodbye. It all had to do with a woman Dad had been dating before he met Mom. This old prom queen had resurfaced like a bad penny, and Mom and Dad had had a fight that Leslie and I pieced together without knowing the details. Now, Leslie's and my worst nightmare was coming true. We shouldn't have been surprised. Mom was always the practical one, thinking about the future and wanting stability. Dad was a loser in that department, although he did seem to be trying to make a go of being an adult when he'd bought the garage in Springhills. So far, he said, it was keeping him in doughnut and coffee money.

How could Dad even hope to compete with old man Putterman, a lawyer, a man born as dependable as a Swiss clock? It made me a little crazy just thinking about it. Heading to Hawk's Creek to stay with my Grandma Connelly seemed an even better idea after I'd heard Mom's news. That was the exact moment when I'd decided not to come back to Springhills. I would live with Grandma Connelly and never come back. The thought of living with a stepfather was more than I could stomach. I looked over at Leslie's bowed head. I was going to miss my little sister, but the thought of living in Hawk's Creek was like a bucket of chocolate chip mint ice cream on a hot summer day.

*   *   *

It was two weeks after Mom's big announcement of doom. Ambie and I were lying on her bed eating bowls of raspberry yogurt the day before I was to fly out to Thunder Bay. Ambie was used to me being away for most of July, and this year, she had slotted herself into a two-week computer camp and a one-week "math is fun" camp.

"Mom was threatening to send me to sports camp, so I signed myself up in computer and math." Ambie grimaced at the thought of physical exertion. "I've saved coaches everywhere from taking early retirement." I laughed, and

Ambie pulled herself up into a sitting position. Her voice became quiet. "Sorry about your mom marrying Putterman. I was really starting to think your dad had a chance." Ambie's hand rested for a moment on my back.

"Yeah, I guess." I sort of wasn't in the mood to talk about the decline of my life. Ambie understood. Since we'd been friends forever, we knew sometimes it was better to let things be.

"Well, your Grandma Connelly will be glad to see you." Ambie sounded sort of wistful. She twined a long piece of her blonde hair around and around in her fingers. "My grandmother never got over Mom divorcing my real father, and they aren't all that close even now. Grandmother's religion forbids sins like divorce, but if you ask me, religion might be better off promoting forgiveness instead of the stay-mad-forever stuff." Ambie released her coiled hair in one sharp movement and hugged herself like she was suddenly cold.

"You're so right, Ambie. This is one screwy world we live in. Do you still think about finding your dad?" Ambie had talked about tracking him down ever since I'd met her.

"Yeah, sometimes. Mom makes him sound like Attila the Hun or a Russian spy who betrayed the free world. She won't talk about him at all. It's like he never existed."

"Well, he must have, or you wouldn't be here. That's one thing we can be sure of." I noticed the time on Ambie's yellow and black happy-face clock. I scraped my spoon all around my bowl, licked the last smears of yogurt off the spoon and jumped to the floor.

"Time to make like a banana and split," I said. I tried to sound cheerier than I felt.

Ambie groaned. "I hope you learn some better lines up north."

"I'll see what I can do. It'll be hard to find someone who grimaces as well as you do."

I gave Ambie a big hug on her front steps. "I'll write every week."

"Me too." That made us both laugh, because we said that every summer and never, ever wrote. Not to mention my grandma didn't have a computer, so e-mail was out.

"Well, see you in August, Jen," Ambie called as I reached the end of her sidewalk.

I kept my head down and kicked a pebble out into the street. Would I be back in August? "Have a good summer, Ambie," I called back and waved.

I slowly walked the six blocks home to Maple Lane, breathing in the fragrance of wild roses still in bloom. The lawns were a little yellow and parched-looking because of the dry spring. I'd heard there'd been a lot of forest fires in Northern Ontario, but so far, they were quite a bit further north than Grandma Connelly's. She lived on a small lake, a few kilometres to the north of Lake Superior. Her house was really a renovated summer camp, or cottage as we call it in Southern Ontario, that she had insulated for winter, with a bedroom and bigger kitchen added on. Leslie and I shared the original bedroom on our visits. Ever since she'd moved to Hawk's Creek, Leslie and I had flown for a visit every summer, and I thought of it as a haven away from the chaos of our real lives.

I had my head down, thinking about Grandma Connelly, when Pete Flaghert fell into step beside me. I was taller than him after shooting up to five eight very suddenly that winter, but now I noticed Pete had me by a couple of inches. He seemed kind of skinny, and his brown hair was a bit shaggy, but his smile was still sweet. Pete and I had gone on a few walks together since the fall, when he'd helped me through a tough time. Once, he'd even had supper at our house when Mom had invited him in. Still, he was often seen hanging about with Angela Frost, and everyone said they were going together. He probably thought I was below the dating scale, since he was going into Grade Twelve, while I was just entering Grade Ten. The thought of Angela and Pete as a couple bothered me.

"I hear you're heading into blackfly country." He gave me a sideways grin. "How long you gone for?"

"Three weeks, I guess," I told him. "I'm toying with the idea of staying with my grandma for good." I don't know why those words just popped out. I immediately wished I could pop them right back in.

Pete stopped walking and turned to face me.

"What's so bad that you don't want to come back?"

"Oh, Mom's just decided to marry Putterman, I barely passed Grade Nine and..." I made an attempt to keep the misery out of my voice, "I like having blackflies suck the blood out of me. It's called the northern diet—way better than counting calories. Every pint is equal to a triple fudge sundae."

I'd never noticed before that Pete's grimace looked a lot like Ambie's. "There's no question your life has had a few glitches, but how could you even think about missing Grade Ten at Morton T. High? That's the year Miss Dragot brings the American Revolution to life with a slide show of each and every bloodstained battle field. The dragon lady talks about the thrill of killing with muskets and bayonets in loving detail. She cheers for the South, by the way, and believe me, she's not happy about the outcome of the uprising." Pete punched me lightly on the arm. "Besides, how will the volleyball team get by without you?"

I shifted from one foot to the other. "Yeah, well, while I'm sure Grade Ten promises to be a not-to-be-missed year and all," I kept my voice light, "I don't really know what I'm going to do yet."

Pete started walking. "I was hoping you'd go to the opening dance with me."

"I thought...that is, aren't you going with Angela?" I felt a flicker of hope.

"We decided to see other people," Pete said, not

sounding too broken up. He stopped walking at the foot of my driveway, looked in my face for a minute, then lightly kissed me on the mouth before setting off down Maple Lane at a half-jog. I stood staring after him with my eyes wide open and my mouth forming an "oh" of surprise.

"See you in a month, Bannon!" he called back over his shoulder. I lifted my hand in a feeble half-wave, all the time thinking that I'd never wash my lips again. Had Pete really made a date with me for the first dance of the year? I gave my head a little shake and practically skipped up the sidewalk to our front steps.

When I slammed the front door behind me, I could hear Mom on the phone in the kitchen. She came into the hall, still holding the receiver to her ear. She was dressed in coveralls and had her hair tied back with a kerchief, so I knew she'd been doing her weekly clean-up. She motioned for me to come nearer and watched me while she talked. Her voice didn't sound particularly friendly.

"Here she is now. Yes, she's packed and we're all set for tomorrow. Okay, I'll call you when I hear she's made it." Mom handed me the phone and mouthed, "Your father," before she walked past me and continued on down the hall to the living room.

"Hi, Jenny bear." Dad's voice sounded tired. I knew he'd been working extra-long hours since he'd heard of Mom's engagement to Putterman. I also knew he was disappointed that I had opted not to work for him for the summer. I felt like I wasn't able to be there for him or for Leslie, because there was just a black hole of panic whenever I thought about Mom marrying someone else. It was easier to push Dad and Leslie away and not think about what was happening to all of us.

"I'm sorry I won't be able to see you tonight before you go. I'm working on this guy's car that has to be ready first thing tomorrow morning. As it is, I'm going to be here until midnight."

"That's okay, Dad."

"Well, I'd really like to have seen you before you left." He paused. "Jennifer?"

"Yeah, Dad?"

"I just want you to know I'm not upset that you decided to go to Grandma's for July. If you want to work for me in August, I'll have some coveralls washed and pressed with your name on them."

"I'll keep that in mind."

"I might even pay you too," he laughed.

"Now you're making an offer that's hard to resist. If you promise to teach me how to drive, I might just take you up on your deal."

He sounded serious all of a sudden. "Any time. If you ever need anything, all you have to do is ask. I'll be here for you when you get back, kiddo."

I didn't want to tell him that I didn't plan to be back for August. "I'll talk to you soon, Dad. You never know. I might even write!"

Dad chuckled, because he knew I wasn't much for writing letters. "I'll miss you. See you next month." He hung up quickly, and I slowly replaced the receiver, feeling a tightness in my throat. It really would be better to get out of Springhills. I couldn't let myself forget that.

*   *   *

The next morning, Mom, Leslie and I ate a nourishing breakfast of dry Fruit Loops washed down with root beer. We'd finished the milk off at suppertime. Mom looked a little sheepish and promised Leslie that they'd stop for groceries on the way home from taking me to the airport. Putterman had lent Mom his car to see me safely off, and by eleven o'clock, we were on our way to Pearson Airport in Toronto. The Fruit Loops and root beer were sloshing around in my stomach, adding to that queasy feeling you get when you have to say goodbye to people you love. Leslie and I sat in the back seat and had a staring contest to see who could make the other laugh first. I won, as usual. Leslie always crumbles when I cross my eyes and puff out my cheeks like a demented chipmunk.

Then, suddenly we were in the terminal, my bag was checked, I passed through security and found myself alone, waiting to board the plane. A flight attendant touched me on the shoulder and led me down the corridor to the plane, settling me in a window seat in row one. I knew that I was getting the young-child-travelling-alone treatment. My mom had to be behind this somewhere. How can someone make you warm and exasperated at the same time?

As I settled back in my seat, my mind was going a hundred miles a minute. I was thinking about the break-up of my parents and, while I wouldn't admit it to Leslie, was still clinging to a childish hope that we could go back to a time when my parents had all the answers. Was I running away from my problems, or was I running towards something better? Would Grandma Connelly let me stay with her longer than three weeks? Too many unresolved questions spun around and around in my head. As the plane taxied down the runway, I was unaware that this was the beginning of the summer that was to change me forever, in ways that I could never begin to imagine.

Two

Grandma Connelly was not in the viewing area when I got off the plane. I waited for a few minutes just inside the door of the airport lounge before following the other passengers to the baggage claim area. The first of the luggage was just beginning to make its journey down the conveyor belt when I found a spot to stand between a woman jiggling a baby in her arms and an older couple dressed in matching Hawaiian shirts. As usual, my two bags were the last to appear. I was reaching for my second suitcase when I heard my name announced over the loudspeaker. "Jennifer Bannon, please report to the information desk." I had a feeling it wasn't going to be good news.

A flaming red-haired woman in a gold airport uniform greeted me with a smile. "Jennifer Bannon? Your grandmother sent that fellow named Jimmy over there to drive you home." She pointed over my right shoulder. "Your grandmother said to tell you that she'll explain why when she sees you."

I turned around and saw a guy dressed in

blue jeans and a black T-shirt watching me. He looked to be in his late teens. He had jet black hair cut long and intense blue eyes set in a brown face. Except for his eyes, I'd have thought he was aboriginal. He slowly came towards me, his arm extended for my bag.

"I'm Jimmy." His voice was low, and I had to lean forward to hear him. "My truck's out this way."

I hurried to keep pace with his long strides. "Why didn't Grandma come to pick me up?" I spoke into his shoulder blades, almost stumbling into him as I lunged forward to get close enough to hear his response.

He half-turned, without slowing down. "She's at home, waiting for you."

I thought he might give me more information about Grandma Connelly, but he didn't speak again for some time.

His truck turned out to be a rusty pickup, dirty on the outside and messy on the inside. I climbed into the front seat after pushing a plastic coffee cup and various food and gum wrappers onto the floor and sat squeezed in beside a tackle box. Jimmy glanced at me as I made a space for myself, and I thought I saw a smile at the corners of his mouth before he turned the key in the ignition. He put the stick shift into gear, and we were soon driving out of the parking lot and onto Highway 17. I decided that two could play the silence game.

After about half an hour of being lulled by the

noise of the engine and the wind blowing through Jimmy's open window, I let out a satisfied sigh. I was becoming reacquainted with the miles of bush and towering rock cuts that were broken up by magnificent views of Lake Superior. Today, the sun made the lake shimmer like a coat of diamonds. I loved these long stretches of wilderness that made me forget about suburbia.

Jimmy spoke for the first time. "Keep your eyes open for moose and deer."

I turned away from the side window and looked at him. "Have there been many accidents?"

He nodded. His blue eyes flicked over me. His black eyelashes had to be about a centimetre long. His cheek bones were high and the angles in his face gave him an exotic look. I swallowed and asked again, "Why couldn't Grandma Connelly come get me?"

Jimmy acted as if he didn't hear me. His head turned as he glanced out the back window. The truck slowed suddenly, and the tires hit the gravel along the side of the highway. He slowly backed up a bit and stopped the truck, pointing to a shadowy spot in the bush. As my eyes adjusted, I saw a mother deer standing perfectly still with her spotted white fawn at her side. They looked right at us before the mother turned away. The fawn watched us for a few seconds more, then I saw flashes of their white tails as they bounded into the brush. In an instant, they had disappeared into the deeper darkness of the woods.

"Wow!" I felt a little leap in my chest. I turned to Jimmy. "Thanks for stopping. I've never been so close to a wild deer before. That was awesome."

Jimmy nodded and pulled the truck back onto the highway. After a few minutes of driving, he spoke as if nothing had happened. "Your Grandma had a slight heart attack last week. It seemed better to let her rest. I offered to come get you. She didn't want you to worry. You know how she is." Jimmy spit the sentences out like watermelon seeds.

The suddenness of his words after such a long silence startled me. I almost thought he was making it up, but I asked automatically, "Is she all right?"

"Yeah, I was with her when it happened and took her to the hospital in town. The doc says she just needs to rest a bit. He said she was lucky this time, 'cause it was more of a warning than anything."

I started to believe him. Still, the meaning of his words took a moment to sink in. Grandma Connelly seemed ageless to me. She was never sick, and I couldn't picture her in the hospital. My enjoyment of the drive was gone, as a feeling of worry and unease settled in my chest. As if sensing my distress, or just to keep me from asking questions, Jimmy turned on the radio and turned it to the country and western station. Normally, I'm not much of a fan, but that afternoon, it didn't matter what we were listening to. For the rest of the ride, I looked out the window and tried not to think about anything.

An hour later, we pulled off the highway onto the dirt road to Hawk's Creek. The road wasn't very wide after the first kilometre or so, and was flanked by shrubs and pine trees that sometimes made you feel like you were driving through a tunnel. Now and then, we'd pass an outcropping of rock and stretches of swamp— good mosquito-breeding ground. A few more kilometres in, we rounded a turn in the road and climbed a steep hill rutted with stones. On the level ground again, I spotted two Native girls playing with dolls on the grass next to the road. They both jumped up, their black hair flying, hands outstretched and waving happily as we drove by. I waved back, and Jimmy trailed his arm out the window in a long salute. I noticed a smile for the first time settling on his face.

"My sisters," he said, and I thought he sounded proud.

I answered without thinking. "They're *so* cute. What're their names?"

Jimmy looked over as if sizing me up. "Marilyn is the eight-year-old, and Doris is five." He gave an odd laugh, almost a cough. "My mother named us after famous people. I'm James Dean Musquash, and there's Marilyn Monroe Musquash and Doris Day Musquash."

He glanced at me again, I suppose waiting for my reaction. I shrugged my shoulders.

"There's worse people to be named after." Actually, I wasn't sure if James Dean was an actor or someone who made sandwiches at Subway. All those famous people were before my time.

"Are there any more kids?" I asked.

Jimmy hesitated before answering. "Just my sister, Audrey Hepburn Musquash. She's sixteen." After that, he clamped his mouth shut and didn't talk any more. I wondered if he was always so hard to get along with.

It didn't matter though, because within minutes, he'd made a quick right turn into my grandma's driveway, or rather clearing, and I leapt out of the truck as soon as it stopped. Suddenly, I couldn't wait to see my grandma, to know that she was all right. I ran down the incline to the back door and practically fell over myself rushing into her living room.

Grandma Connelly was sitting in a recliner, and on her face was a huge smile. Her arms were opened wide to welcome me. I hugged her warmth carefully, because I was worried about hurting her. Grandma's arms seemed frailer than I remembered, but she hugged me back firmly.

"I'm sorry that I couldn't meet your plane. Did Jimmy tell you...?" She stopped speaking as she saw Jimmy enter with my bag. I turned and saw him nod to my grandma, and she continued. "Well now, you two must be hungry, so help yourselves to those sandwiches and pops that are waiting in the fridge. I know the airlines don't feed you much any more, and I bet Jimmy never stopped for anything to eat along the way." She smiled gently at us both.

Jimmy and I looked at each other, and I said, "I'll get it," as I crossed to the fridge to pull out the food and drinks.

"It's so good to have you here, Jennifer," Grandma said. "No, none for me right now. I'll eat later. I guess you must be tired after that long drive and all. I'm kind of tired myself today, so I'm just going to go for a sleep. Then we'll have a nice long chat."

I noticed that the creases around Grandma's eyes were deeper than I remembered. Jimmy went over and helped Grandma up from her chair, but she refused to let him help her any further. "Make yourself at home, Jenny girl, and put your stuff in the old bedroom. It's too bad Leslie didn't make it this trip. I'll see you in a bit." Grandma walked stiffly the short distance to her bedroom and waved before softly closing her door. I heard the bed springs squeak as she lay down.

Jimmy finished his sandwich in a few gulps and headed for the back door with his can of pop. His silence was starting to bug me.

"Thanks for coming to get me." I figured I owed him something, even if he didn't act like I was on the radar screen.

He turned and nodded again, but this time

he didn't look at me. I thought he said, "See you around," when the screen door slammed, but it might easily have been something else.

The little house was just as I remembered it. The walls were lined in pine, and Grandma's artwork covered most of the available space. She painted beautiful, rugged images of the north as well as its wildlife. I especially liked her painting of a mother black bear and her cubs in a clearing in the woods. The kitchen and living room were not really separated, making the whole place open but cosy at the same time. A huge stone fireplace filled one wall, and Grandma also had a potbellied stove for heat near her recliner. On the other side of the stove was an old couch that was covered by a Hudson's Bay blanket. A wooden rocker and some overflowing bookcases completed the room. On either side of the front door were two huge windows that looked out at a grove of birch and pine trees and the lake beyond. While Grandma had electricity, she often lit the fire and kerosene lamps at night just because she liked the atmosphere better.

I grabbed my suitcases from near the door and lugged them as quietly as possible into the spare bedroom. I could still smell the faint mustiness of turpentine and paint, since Grandma used this room as her painting studio when nobody was visiting. In the summer, she usually painted outdoors and kept her stuff in a shed behind the cottage.

The same bunk beds that I remembered were along one wall beside an open window. Grandma had placed a reading lamp on a little table beside my bed. I smiled to see a vase of daisies and buttercups next to the lamp. On the other side of the window were a chest of drawers, emptied for my use, and a little closet that was packed with Grandma's things.

I quickly unpacked my suitcases, finding lots of room in the chest of drawers. I tested the bottom bunk, then figured I might as well explore outside. I crossed the living room and stepped out into a world of lengthening shadows as the sun settled behind the pine trees. The smell of pine needles and warm earth made me pause for a moment and take a deep breath. All that fresh, clean, northern air should get rid of the city smog.

My feet led me down the narrow path to the lake and Grandma's dock. Her beach was mostly rock and not much sand, but the lake dropped off sharply so that your feet didn't touch the bottom for very long. I remembered that the water didn't heat up enough for swimming until the end of the summer. Still, in summers past, Leslie and I had swum every day, ignoring the pins and needles in our legs and arms when we first jumped in. Grandma had a new dock, I noticed, and her little motor boat was tied up alongside. It reminded me of the many hours that Leslie and I had spent puttering around the lake in that boat, looking for fish and exciting shoreline to explore. I was going to miss my little sister more than I had thought.

I crouched near the end of the dock and stared into the depths below. The waves lapped gently against the boat, and I felt a sense of calm, but also sadness. As if to echo my mood, a loon called hauntingly across the water. I felt a strange desire to cry, but I had given that up some time ago. Tears get you nowhere.

I squatted for a while before dangling my legs over the side of the dock. I stared across the lake and positioned myself so I could watch the sun disappear behind the pines. Just as the last of the light was fading and I was thinking about heading back to the cottage, I heard a branch crack behind me, somewhere off to my right. I spun around and tried to peer into the shadows and bushes in the direction of the sound. I could see nothing. Still, I had a creepy feeling that someone was watching me. I called out, "Who's there?" but my voice hung in the silence.

I ran across the dock and up the path that was by now getting quite dark. I felt the hairs on the back of my neck standing up, and my feet couldn't take me up the path fast enough. I sort of fell into the cottage, which was also in darkness. Grandma was still sleeping, and I had forgotten to turn on the lights before I'd gone outside. I fumbled for the wall switch, and the room jumped into light. I hesitated inside the door, feeling disoriented, and wondered fearfully if somebody was outside looking in through a window. "Get a grip, Jennifer Bannon!" I ordered, and forced myself to close the curtains on every window to shut out the night and prying eyes.

Was I just imagining things because I was overtired, or was there really somebody watching me? I gave myself a shake and decided that all I needed was a good night's sleep. The stress of the day was doing bad things to my tired but overactive imagination. I reminded myself that Hawk's Creek was a place where nothing bad ever happened.

Three

I awoke the next morning to a room still in semi-darkness and the sounds of my grandma making breakfast in the kitchen. I lay quietly for a moment, listening to her humming what I knew was her favourite song of all time, "A Little Help From My Friends". She loved the Beatles and knew every one of their songs by heart. I was suddenly glad I'd come to spend the summer with her.

I jumped out of bed and rustled around in the drawers for a sweater to put on over my nightgown. The one I pulled out was an emerald green cable knit that hung to my knees. My grandmother had knitted it for my mother when she was a teenager. It was pretty worn-looking, with the odd snag, but I liked wearing it just fine. Happily, Grandma didn't have a mirror in the room, so I didn't have to look at my grumpy morning face. I knew my blonde hair must look like I'd stuck my finger in a light socket. It was down past my shoulders and longer than I liked to wear it.

As I entered the kitchen, Grandma met me

with a glass of orange juice and a hug. She motioned for me to sit where she'd laid out a bowl of cereal and a homemade bran muffin. Neither of us was much for talking first thing in the morning, and we gladly ignored each other until we'd eaten. Still, I kept an eye on her when she didn't know I was looking. It troubled me that she only nibbled at a piece of toast and sipped a weak cup of tea. Her hand shook a bit when she held the cup to her lips, and I had to look away because Grandma wasn't someone who ever wanted sympathy or to be fussed over. Still, I couldn't stop myself from worrying that she was sicker than she was letting on.

I cleared our cups and bowls from the table and filled the sink with soapy water. I was rolling up my sleeves to do the dishes when Grandma put her hand on my shoulder.

"Leave those for now. Come sit with me and tell me all about your foolish mother and father and my darling Leslie," she commanded, walking into the living room and stretching out in her old leather chair. I followed and half-lay on the couch so that I was facing her. I began to fill her in on the details of life in Springhills.

"Leslie has discovered the ballet, and next to her guinea pig Puffball, it's all she talks about. Mom is getting a lot of shifts at the hospital, and Dad...well, Dad's busy with his garage. He still needs to build up his customers, but I know he will. He's a really good mechanic." I didn't want Grandma to think badly of him.

Grandma said, "So, she's going to marry John Putterman." She shook her head back and forth a few times. "I never could tell that girl anything. Your father hurt her, you know, and Alice just doesn't get over that kind of thing easily. She's got my stubborn streak, I'm afraid."

I'd wondered if Mom had told Grandma her engagement news. Now I knew. "Do you think there's any hope for Dad? I mean, he's really trying to make up for hurting us, but Mom keeps getting mad at him. It's like she can't stop punishing him." I bit my bottom lip and looked at Grandma to see if she thought I had it all wrong.

Grandma reached for my hand and rubbed it between her own two. "Oh, my Jennifer. You are beginning to understand the workings of the wounded. Your mother can't forgive your father, because her pride won't let her."

"Wouldn't it be better to forget about pride and let us be a family again?"

Grandma's eyes were gentle, but her voice was matter-of-fact. "Alice never takes the easy road."

Suddenly, I didn't want to talk about my parents any more. It was easy to get Grandma to change the subject by asking her about the Musquashes. "What's Jimmy's family like?"

Grandma let go of my hand and leaned back in her recliner. "Well, they moved in late last summer, a few weeks after you and Leslie went back home. I have an artist friend who lives further north in Pike Lake, and she said there was some unpleasantness there concerning the Musquashes. The police were involved, and things got ugly. Seems there was stealing going on and...well...you know how people are. They like to blame people different from themselves. The mom, Connie Musquash, is aboriginal, and her husband Ed is white, so that makes the kids a mixture of races. I've heard some of our nastier neighbours call them half-breeds. I'm afraid I sometimes despair of the human race." Grandma reached down and pulled her knitting from a bag beside her chair. It looked like she was halfway through making a sapphire blue sweater, but it was too small for me or Leslie to wear.

"Who's that for?" I asked.

"Oh, little Doris Musquash. I'm making both of the younger Musquash girls sweaters for their birthdays." Grandma looked thoughtful as her needles settled into a steady rhythm of clicks.

"If Mr. Musquash is white, why does he have an aboriginal last name?" I asked.

"Oh, I hear he was adopted by a native family when he was a baby. I'm not too sure of the facts, but Jimmy once told me that his father grew up in the far north. Jimmy is eighteen and has been helping me out. Did you see the dock he built this spring?"

I nodded.

Grandma continued, "He's quiet, but sometimes he brings Marilyn and Doris over, and he's as kind with them as anything. I'd hate to think he was the one who got the family in trouble. Then there's Audrey..." Grandma's knitting stopped for a moment. "She's a hard one to pin down. I've seen her around a bit, and she seems kind of lost. The neighbours say she's trouble through and through. I don't know." Grandma gave me a smile. "Well, that's enough gossip for one day. I hate repeating things others say, but I guess you should be aware of the state of things. Anyhow, make up your own mind about people and don't listen to gossip. I'd like to see the community give them a chance."

Grandma had always encouraged us to be open-minded and to speak up for ourselves. You always knew where you stood with her, which I can't say about too many other people.

"Grandma, is that old hermit guy still living back in the woods?"

Grandma nodded. "Joe—that's his name, by the way—has taken to building bird feeders and birdhouses, and his property is covered with them. You might have noticed I have a few on the pines out back." She paused for a second before changing the subject. "Oh, here's something of interest. The Randalls have been back and forth from town, and Kerry's been asking for you."

Kerry was my age, and she had a little brother Freddie, who was ten. Leslie and I had spent a lot of time with them when we were visiting in past summers. This news cheered me somewhat. "Grandma, I think I might go for a walk down the road. Can I do anything for you before I leave?"

Grandma shook her head. "I'm just fine here with my knitting. You run along and get some exercise before the weather turns bad."

It was a grey kind of day, and a little chilly with the clouds threatening rain. After doing the dishes, I dressed in shorts, sneakers and an oversized sweatshirt. I managed to pull my hair back into a ponytail and put on a Yankees baseball cap that I found hanging on a hook by the back door. I knew it wouldn't take me long to warm up once I got running.

I jogged down the dirt road, heading away from the main highway. Mr. Jacks, my volleyball coach, had told us to cross-train over the summer to be ready for fall tryouts. He said that nobody should consider their place on the team a sure thing. I guess I hadn't gotten through my mind that I wasn't going back to Springhills. It was going to take a major shift in thought patterns. Still, I felt as if I was waiting for some sign from above to let me know what I should do. Maybe Grandma's heart attack was a sign that she needed me. Then, there was Pete inviting me to the fall dance. Maybe that was a sign I should go home. I was beginning to think the higher power was messing with my mind.

I slowed my pace and started to notice the woods around me. Brush began near the road—

what appeared to be raspberry bushes mixed up with thorn bushes and sapling alders. Behind were spruce and pines with their lower branches looking like spindly arms that hadn't grown properly. I raised my eyes above the tree line and saw a hawk circling overhead. Picking up my speed again, I rounded a bend. I had my head down, watching that I didn't step in any potholes. The dirt road was more rutted and uneven than I remembered and would probably need a road crew to fix it up before much longer. I glanced up.

At first I thought I saw a dark shadow rising up from a big rock some distance away from the road, but my heart leapt in fright when the shadow gradually took on the form of a person. I thought about turning around and making the hundred-yard dash home, but figured that might be just too paranoid. Instead, I slowed my jog to a walk, still thinking I could get away if I had to, while trying to see, without looking obvious, who was sitting on the rock. That's hard to do when you're alone on a dirt road with nothing much else to look at. I came alongside just as I happily realized that the person was a girl, a little older than me, with straight black hair to her waist, large black eyes and brown skin. She was dressed in tight cutoff shorts and a white T-shirt. I thought she was quite pretty, but when she spoke, her mouth and eyes mocked me. She threw out her words like a challenge. "You must be that old lady's granddaughter here from the *big* city." She pulled a flattened pack of cigarettes from her back pocket. "Come join me for a smoke, city girl."

I stopped walking and shook my head. Mr. Jacks would kick me off every school team forever if I took up smoking. Thinking about going back to Springhills was like a habit I couldn't shake. "You must be Jimmy's sister, Audrey. My name's Jennifer. My friends call me Jen."

Audrey said, "Aren't you scared of being a social outcast talking to a half-breed like me, *Jen*?" She took a long drag on her cigarette and watched me with narrowed eyes through the smoke as she exhaled.

"I guess that doesn't bother me much." I kept my eyes level with hers, "if it doesn't bother you."

Audrey stared at me without blinking for a few moments. Then she jumped off the rock, throwing down her cigarette onto the road and grinding it out with her sandal. "Do you want to see a beaver dam?"

I felt like I had passed some kind of test. "That'd be great."

I followed her along a narrow path through the bushes on the other side of the road. Insects buzzed around our heads and followed us into the undergrowth like a parade. We had to clear branches from the path as we went, and Audrey was careful not to let any snap back into my face. She was sure-footed and led me around fallen tree limbs and over rocks as effortlessly as if she were walking down a city street. I felt awkward and tried to keep pace, breathing harder than Mr. Jacks would have liked. I was definitely going to have to start working out more if I was going to make that volleyball team.

After about fifteen minutes, and just as I was beginning to wonder if Audrey was leading me on a wild goose chase, we reached a clearing of rocks and bulrushes opening into a greyish-brown pond. She pointed to a dark, muddy mound at one end where the pond narrowed. Brown branches and twigs stuck out of the pile like a bad hair day. "Watch closely, and we should see a beaver."

We squatted down in the dirt. Sure enough, before five minutes had passed, a huge beaver swam towards the middle of the pond, holding a tree limb in its teeth. The water parted like a triangle in its wake. Audrey sat absolutely still and watched with intense concentration. The warmth of her bare arm rested against my own where I'd pushed up the sleeve of my sweatshirt. I saw her smile and glance at me to see if I was pleased with the gift she was offering me. At that moment, I decided that I liked her.

"Are you happy living in Hawk's Creek?" I asked her softly, not wanting to ruin this moment of closeness. Audrey didn't move except to pull her arm away from my own.

"It'll do." She breathed out the words tonelessly, without emotion. After another moment, she said,

"Jimmy is leaving tomorrow for a job in the bush. He says he'll be back on the weekends." She pulled her hair away from her face in a swift motion.

I thought a flicker of fear crossed her face, but at the time, I thought I must be mistaken. She stood up quickly, tossing back her hair and said, "Come on, city girl. I'll get you back to the main road."

I stood from my crouching position and stretched my cramped legs. Audrey was already disappearing into the woods.

Our trek back seemed quicker than our walk to the pond. Before long, I could see the road through the brush.

"Thanks for taking me, Audrey. I hope we can do something together again," I said.

She half-turned and her black eyes brushed over mine. "I might see you around," she said. "You never know."

She left me at the end of the path and started running the opposite way down the road. Her long black hair was like a stream of ink behind her. She ran like a gazelle with strides long and fluid, but she ran so fast that it looked like she was being chased by demons. I watched her for a long time, and she never once looked back. For some reason, a shiver of loneliness travelled up from my belly. Why were Jimmy and Audrey so difficult to get to know? What was the secret of the Musquash family? It was too bad Ambie wasn't there to talk things over with. She would have understood how I was feeling without being asked. Maybe I'd break tradition and write to her after all. I sighed. Ambie was probably having a great time at computer camp and had hardly noticed that I was gone.

As I turned for home, the first drops of rain began to strike the leaves of the trees, and before I reached the turn in the road, the whole world was alive with the music of the storm. I too started running, only I felt like I was running towards some place warm and safe. As for Audrey, I wasn't so sure.

Four

The days settled into a pattern of not much to do and lots of time to do it in. I started sleeping in until midmorning, usually finding a note on the table from Grandma that she was out painting and would be back before supper. A few days after I arrived, she said that she was feeling stronger and didn't want to waste the good weather inside being an invalid. She drove an old Jeep—if that didn't mark a lifestyle change from her city life, I don't know what did—and managed to get to some pretty out-of-the-way places. I told her this worried me, since she'd been sick and all, but she promised to keep close to some well-travelled areas. She said that the great thing about the North is that you didn't have to stray far to find a view worth painting. Grandma also told me that she was scheduled to put on an art show in Thunder Bay towards the end of the summer, and she needed a couple more pieces. So, I swallowed that little, niggling worry about her health and let myself turn into a sloth.

About a week after I got to Hawk's Creek, a

boat carrying Kerry Randall and her brother Freddie arrived at our dock. It was just after lunch on a rather cool but sunny day, and I must say that I was beginning to get tired of the book I'd been reading. I was also starting to get a bit bored after my week of doing nothing. Grandma was usually home by four o'clock, and by then I was salivating for some company. Kerry and Freddie, waving and calling to me from the middle of the lake, were a welcome sight.

Kerry was one of those outgoing, popular girls who usually make homecoming queen. She once told me that her goal in life was to be a dancer on a cruise ship after she won some major beauty contests. She was blonde like me, but bubblier and more self-confident. I sometimes thought she was performing for a hidden camera that only she could see. She could get on my nerves, but most of the time, we got along okay.

Her brother, Freddie, was a chubby, redheaded little kid whose only interests were eating and looking for frogs and bugs. He had freckles all over his face and the biggest cowlick I'd ever seen, next to Dennis the Menace. He got along with his sister by ignoring her and barely acknowledged my existence either. Kerry liked to tell him that their parents had brought the wrong baby home from the hospital and not to get too comfortable.

Once they'd tied the boat at our dock and climbed ashore, we climbed the path up to the cottage so they could look around. Freddie trailed behind us through the front door into the living room.

"Your grandma's done the place up nice," said Kerry. "I remember what a dump it used to be before she moved in. I really like the pine floors. *So* rustic."

Freddie spun his pointer fingers around his temples like she was crazy and said, "I'm bored. Got any food?"

"Sure thing," I said, heading for the kitchen.

I fed him a handful of Oreo cookies, gave him a bucket and fish net, and he headed down to the dock. That left Kerry and me curled up in the deck chairs under the pine tree drinking lemonade. Every so often, she would toss her hair back and flash her beauty contestant smile in my direction.

"It's just *so good* to have you back. You look *so* pretty in that red T-shirt with your face all tanned." She sighed dramatically. "Too bad Leslie isn't here too to keep that rotten brother of mine out of our hair."

I couldn't imagine how she thought Freddie could be any less in our hair. He was lying on the end of the dock, scooping whatever drifted by into a pail. I'd forgotten how much Kerry liked to gossip, so I was surprised when she began telling me stories about people who lived in town. Most of the people I didn't know, and I was beginning to think I was glad I didn't know them, when Kerry started talking about the Musquashes.

"Can you imagine anyone wearing those little

tank tops and shorts up to...well, you know where!" I'd been drifting in and out of her monologue, and it took me a minute to clue in that she was referring to Audrey.

"Her reputation couldn't get much lower. Like, all the boys think she's a..." Kerry whispered an insult to me on the off-chance that Freddie, who was about three blocks away from us, might overhear.

I didn't know what to say, so I just looked at Kerry and frowned.

Kerry continued without noticing I wasn't too happy about what she was saying. "Audrey was caught stealing back where she came from, and there was something about her and a teacher. Mr. Musquash told Luke Tanner, you know the guy I just told you about who has two wives? Anyhow, Mr. Musquash told him that they had to move because of the teacher and what Audrey had done. Like, nobody knows the whole story, but everybody has their own ideas. I think Audrey Musquash is just bad news." Kerry's blonde hair tossed back and forth in disapproval.

I started to feel guilty at my own silence. I'd opened my mouth to tell her that I didn't want to hear any more when she started talking again.

"Now, Jimmy," she leaned closer, "my, oh my, he's one sweet-looking guy. He dated Tanya Barrett last fall, but not for long. She said he wasn't in touch with his feminine side."

I let out a snort, but Kerry didn't seem to notice.

"He could, like, ask me out all he wants, and I would just say no." She seemed to be quoting the anti-drug campaign slogan.

"Would you like to go for a sw..."

"Freddie! You watch out now!" she screamed before I could finish. She turned back to me and sighed. "He's such a little pig. You're so lucky you don't have a younger brother to drive you completely off the deep end. Why my parents couldn't have stopped at one, I'll never know."

Freddie turned his back on us even further and continued to lean over the dock, swooping his net into the water. At that moment, I missed Leslie more than I can say. She used to be right in there catching tadpoles along with Freddie. I imagined he too was disappointed that she'd stayed in Springhills.

"Mr. Musquash is okay, though," Kerry conceded. "He works for my dad in the winter plowing snow and is custodian at the recreation centre all year. He's always smiling and says hello. Why he ever married that fat Native woman, we'll never know. She's too lazy even to leave her house."

I was sure Kerry thought that she was speaking for the whole town. "Maybe he loves her," I couldn't help saying.

Kerry shook her head again in disapproval. "You're just *too* sweet for words, Jennifer Bannon." She cocked her head and smiled at me like she was humouring a silly child.

I hadn't realized what an airhead she'd become. I didn't even try to argue with her. I figured there was just no point.

In the end, Kerry and I did have a swim, and she was a lot more likable when she started playing and stopped talking about people. We splashed around for a while, but it really was too chilly to stay in for long. After about twenty minutes, we towelled off and went to change in the cottage.

"Do you and Freddie want to stay for supper?" I asked as she gathered up her things into a knapsack.

"Maybe another time, Jen. Mom expects us back by four because we have to drive back to town. Could you come visit next Tuesday? Mom has the week off from her part-time job, and we'll be spending the week at the lake."

"That would be good. Yes, I'll come over in Grandma's boat." It wasn't like I had anything else to do.

"Come for lunch and a swim." She stepped out the front door and called, "Freddie! Come on! It's time to go!"

Freddie was squatting next to the boat, poking a stick into his pail and pretending that the mud brown garter snake on Kerry's seat had gotten there by itself. Kerry didn't notice as she settled herself next to the motor until she felt something slithering across her leg. She nearly capsized the boat trying to get away.

"Freddie, I hate you! I hate you, you little worm!" she screamed at him.

Freddie had wisely chosen to remain safely out of reach on the dock. He turned and looked at me like a satisfied cat and grinned. I couldn't stop myself from grinning back. After one afternoon with Kerry, I was starting to appreciate the kid more and more.

*   *   *

I met Mr. Musquash one morning soon after Kerry's visit. After deciding that sleeping in until nearly noon wasn't a good thing, I had started a two kilometre jog every morning before breakfast. I always ran past the Musquash driveway but never went up their laneway. Usually, Doris and Marilyn were outside, skipping or playing with their dolls. I always waved when I ran by, and they would smile shyly at me. After a few mornings, they began waving back.

A week after I'd started my new exercise regime, I was searching for Doris and Marilyn in their yard as usual, but that morning, they weren't playing anywhere near the road. Instead, Mr. Musquash stood at the end of his property, watching me through his dark sunglasses. He was shorter than me and kind of burly, with a long mustache and a bald head. I couldn't see his eyes, but he smiled and motioned for me to stop. I jogged over to stand beside him.

"Hello there," he said and reached out his hand to shake mine, removing his sunglasses at the same time. "You must be Mrs. Connelly's granddaughter. It's nice to meet you."

"Yes, I'm here for the summer."

"Well, good to see a new young person in the neighbourhood. There aren't many pretty young ladies along this stretch of road." He laughed, and I saw that one of his front teeth was missing. He half-turned towards his house. "See you around, then."

"Yes, see you around," I said and smiled back, noticing Doris's and Marilyn's faces in the window. I waved at them before continuing my jog up the road. I felt Mr. Musquash watching me until I rounded the bend, but he was gone when I returned back that way. It seemed hard to believe that he was Audrey's father. She didn't look like him at all, as far as I could tell. Jimmy, however, had Mr. Musquash's brilliant blue eyes, but where Mr. Musquash's eyes were friendly and smiling, Jimmy's were closed off and hard to read.

*　　*　　*

I'd promised Grandma that I wouldn't go swimming unless someone else was around. Most days, I waited until she came home in the afternoon before having a swim off the end of the dock. Grandma usually joined me, and this became my favourite part of the day. She'd sit on the dock sipping a glass of white wine with her feet in the water. I'd swim to the big rock at the point and back a few times until I got tired. Then Grandma would wade in and float on her back while I treaded water beside her. We talked about everything and nothing. Usually, we found lots to laugh about.

One rather foggy morning, when Grandma had decided to stay in bed, I looked out the living room window and saw someone sitting on the edge of the dock. As I strained my eyes to see, the person stood and skimmed a stone across the lake. It took me a minute to realize that the person was Audrey. I scrambled into my bedroom to change out of my pajamas. By the time I'd put on my sandals and raced outside, Audrey had vanished. I was disappointed.

A few mornings later, I saw Audrey again, lost in thought, crouching at the end of the dock. Again, I was too slow to catch her before she disappeared into the woods. I became determined to reach her before she slipped away, thinking maybe she was too shy to come up to the cottage.

I waited two more mornings, getting up earlier than usual and dressing right away. Finally, my waiting paid off. The third morning Audrey appeared from the woods and walked quietly to the end of the dock, where she stood motionless looking across the bay. I didn't want to startle her, but ran quickly down the path so that she couldn't leave without falling over me.

I was breathless but feeling pleased with myself until I saw the look on Audrey's face. Her eyes were puffy and rimmed in red, as if she'd been crying. The smile on my face must have changed to concern pretty quickly. Then, it was like a camera lens shutting in Audrey's eyes, and all softness vanished.

"Hey, city girl. You here to kick me off your dock?" Her voice mocked me just as it had at our first meeting.

"Actually, I'm glad to see you here," I said. I didn't want to scare her away. "I was hoping you might want to swim with me, because I'm not allowed to swim alone, and you'd be doing me a favour." My words fell all over each other as I tried to keep her from running away.

Audrey looked at me, I think, trying to decide if I was asking out of pity. Finally she answered, "I don't have a suit."

"I have an extra one piece that should fit. It's kind of flowery looking, if you can handle poppies in bloom. Sometimes my fashion sense is sadly lacking."

Audrey gave me a quick smile and said, "Sure, why not? I like poppies."

We ran to the cottage and changed, then raced each other back to the dock. The suit was a little tight on Audrey, but she said it didn't matter. She was a born swimmer, strong and powerful in the water.

"Do you want to race to the point and back?" I asked after a while.

"Sure, if you think you're up to being beaten," she said, grinning.

"Don't count your chickens, Musquash. I was on the school swim team. The front crawl is my specialty."

We were neck in neck at the point, but Audrey made the turn better than I did, and she beat me to the dock by a body length. "You're not bad, Bannon," she said, breathing heavily, "for a city girl. If you'd made the turn better, you might have had me." We'd just pulled ourselves out of the water and onto the dock.

"Thanks," I said, rolling over onto my back so that I could catch my breath. "We'll have to have a rematch another day. Best two out of three."

We got the inner tubes out of the shed and floated around, paddling with our hands. After a while, we started splashing each other, then playing bumper cars with our inner tubes. We screamed and giggled until we pushed each other into the water.

"That was fun," she said when we finally lay on the dock wrapped in beach towels. "I wish we lived on the lake. Your grandma has a great spot."

"We could do this every morning," I proposed. "That is, if you want to."

Audrey's eyes were shining, and she quickly nodded her head. "I'd like that. Are you sure...that is...your grandma won't mind?"

"Grandma was hoping I'd find a swimming

partner. You'd be doing me a favour."

"Okay, city girl. You're on. I'll be back tomorrow morning around eight. I'd better get back home now. I hadn't meant to stay so long."

We went up to the cottage to change. Audrey slipped away before I'd put on my clothes. I called her name but only found the flowered bathing suit and towel neatly folded over a kitchen chair. It was as if she'd never even been there.

Five

I hadn't forgotten about my family back in Springhills. Grandma and I had phoned them the day after I'd arrived and again the following Sunday.

Leslie got on the phone first. "Molly and I were in a fight because she always copies everything I do. Now she has a new best friend—Suzy Collins."

"Hang in there, kiddo, Molly'll come around. Maybe, you can make new friends."

"Yes, I don't need her anyhow."

"How's Mom?"

"She's either working or out with Mr. Putterman." Leslie sounded sulky.

"I wish you were here with me, Leslie. I sure miss you."

"Next summer I'm coming with you for sure. Being a ballerina isn't all it's cracked up to be. My feet hurt. Also, you don't get to wear anything pretty unless you're in a show. I think it's false advertising."

Then Mom got on the line. She sounded distracted. "How's Grandma?"

"She's okay." Grandma had given me specific instructions not to tell Mom about her heart attack. She'd said that Mom would only worry needlessly.

"We miss you. John's been sleeping over while I'm on nights, so Leslie's not alone. Have you booked your flight home?"

"Well, about that. Grandma's invited me to stay a bit longer."

"Oh? I was counting on you to come home and look after Leslie while I'm at work."

It was always about what was easiest for Mom. Poor old Putterman having to babysit. Maybe it was giving him a taste of family life and what he was in for once he married Mom. I started to get mad. She hadn't even asked if I was having a good time. "Actually, I don't know when I'll be home. I'm thinking about staying here and going to school in the fall."

Mom was silent. Finally, she said, "What's going on, Jennifer?"

"Nothing, Mom. You're not the only one who can change the people she wants to live with."

"I'm going to hang up now, Jennifer. I want you to reconsider what you're saying. I'll talk to you next week, and we'll book your flight."

"I told you, Mom. I'm not ready to come home."

I heard the click as she hung up.

I turned and saw Grandma standing in the doorway. The look on her face told me that she had heard everything. She opened her arms and I went to her. She whispered into my ear, "This will work out, my dear. Just give it time."

How could Mom blow our lives apart for good by marrying Putterman? I was filled with a great emptiness that kept threatening to choke me. I felt this anger at my mother that almost made me sick. I knew that she could make us a family again if she wanted to. Besides, whatever happened to that "till death do us part" stuff that Mom and Dad had pledged to each other? Could they decide not to love Leslie and me just as easily? It made me want to run and run away forever.

*   *   *

I had been with Grandma for three weeks, and we were sitting in her hammock side by side after a supper of lake trout, rocking aimlessly and enjoying the evening settling around us. We'd lit some citronella candles to keep the bugs away, and I kept getting whiffs of their lemony scent every time we rocked forward. Grandma seemed a bit tired and said, "I might turn in soon for a good night's sleep. I want to be up early to scout out a new place to begin a final painting for my art show."

I hesitated, but finally asked, "Grandma, do you think I could stay for August too? I bought an open-ended ticket, so I'm not really scheduled to be back on a certain date."

Grandma looked at me in silence for a few moments. Then she smiled and reached for my hand. She said, "Of course, you can stay. That would be delightful. We'll just have to phone your mom to let her know, but I love your company, and nothing would please me more. Don't worry, dear. I know how to bring your mom around."

I had been scared that Grandma would turn me away, since I hadn't asked her before I'd told Mom that I wasn't coming home, and her words lifted something from my heart. I wrapped my arms around her and breathed, "Oh, thank you Grandma. You're the best!"

She patted my back as if she was comforting me, and I heard her say, "You are such a sweet child. Things always work out as they should."

I wanted more than anything to believe her.

*   *   *

Audrey and I had fallen into a morning ritual of meeting on the dock and swimming for an hour every morning. Afterwards, we would sit with our legs dangling in the water off the end of the dock and talk. She didn't seem as tough and loose as everyone said, but still, I was hesitant to ask her anything too personal.

One day, I asked, "What do you do for the rest of the day after you come for a swim?" I never saw her around when I went for a jog later in the morning, and I was curious. Lately, it was just Mr. Musquash who waved at me as I jogged by. He was rebuilding the front steps and had set up a skillsaw near the front door where he cut cedar into boards. I heard the whir of the blade as I neared their house. Once he'd started the project, Marilyn and Doris had stopped playing in the front yard.

Audrey answered, "I go home and clean the house. My mother...she has this condition that keeps her from doing much. Then I usually walk to the highway and hitchhike into town."

"What's wrong with your mom?"

Audrey rested her chin on her knees. Her black hair hung heavily over her shoulder in a braid. "She has a phobia about leaving the house. It didn't used to be so bad, but now she can't even go outside."

"How long has she been like that?"

"The last few years or so."

"Audrey, it's not really safe to be hitchhiking."

"Yeah, well, I'm sick of going into town. Lately, I've been going up to that old hermit's place to help him build birdhouses."

This news surprised me. "Is he friendly?"

Audrey nodded. "Joe doesn't talk much, but he's teaching me about carpentry, and I like it. I guess it's safe enough." She mumbled the last words more to herself than to me.

"Maybe you could take me up there sometime?" I wondered if Joe would mind me being on his property.

Audrey shrugged, "Maybe."

*　　*　　*

One day, at the end of July, Audrey came by but said she didn't feel like swimming. She was wearing jeans and a hooded sweatshirt, even though the day was looking like it would be a hot one.

I was disappointed, having looked forward to a swim. "Are you sick, Audrey?"

Her dark eyes looked into mine, and she shrugged. "Just the monthly curse. I'm really not up to a swim."

This seemed unlike her, but I didn't ask any more. Instead, I said, "Do you want some tea? That might make you feel better."

She looked behind her into the bushes near the road. "Okay. I can stay just a little while." She rubbed her arm like it was sore.

"Have you hurt your arm?"

She dropped her hand. "I walked into a door. Don't worry, it's okay. I'm kind of clumsy." She laughed self-consciously.

"You're not having a very good day," I said. I left her on the dock and went up to make the tea. It took a few minutes for the kettle to boil, and I watched her from the window. She'd squatted on the edge of the dock and was poking in the water with a broken tree branch. She looked deep in thought.

I picked camomile and poured the boiling water into Grandma's periwinkle blue teapot. Balancing the teapot and two mugs painted with butterflies, I walked carefully down to the dock. I had to call Audrey's name twice before she came to the deck chairs to have her tea.

"You seemed a million miles away."

"Yeah, that might be nice." She laughed. It was short and harsh. She blew on her tea. "Jimmy's come home for good. He didn't like the guy he was working for."

"Oh? Does he have anything else lined up?"

"He'll probably work at the diner like he did last summer. He was the short-order cook—you know—making hamburgers and sandwiches and stuff."

I asked, "What about you, Audrey? Do you know what you want to do after high school?"

Audrey's eyes were suddenly dancing. "I've been taking hairdressing courses at high school so I can move to Toronto and work in a shop, maybe even start my own business."

I'd grown so tired of my own hair that I asked, "Can you do something with my hair before I shave myself bald?"

Audrey studied my head, her face interested. "You'd look good with a short, spikier kind of hairstyle, if you want a big change."

"Sounds wonderful. How about tomorrow?"

"Tomorrow? If nothing else comes up, sure. I could do that."

She finished her tea in a few gulps, suddenly seeming jumpy. She looked around a few times before leaping up and saying she had to go.

I was getting used to her sudden departures and sat for a while after she'd left, staring into the woods. Then I collected the dishes and started up the path to the house. When I lifted my head, I thought I saw someone at the window. I knew I was imagining it, because Grandma wouldn't be back until after lunch. I slowed my steps and surveyed the windows. I blinked, and the shadows shifted. Now, the window looked empty and still. Had I been imagining a person standing there? Maybe it was just a trick of light. I shook off my fear and entered the front door, looking around the room and behind the furniture, ready to bolt out the front door if I had to. I shouted "Grandma? Is anybody here? Audrey?" All the time, I kept telling myself that I was being ridiculous. Still, I was really happy that nobody answered my calls.

Letting out a big breath, I bent to pick up the tray from the coffee table where I'd set it when I'd first come into the cabin. I walked towards the kitchen and stopped suddenly in alarm. The cups rattled against each other as I lowered the tray to the counter with shaking hands. I was certain I'd shut the back door after putting the garbage out this morning. Why was the door now swinging gently back and forth in the breeze? I forced myself to step outside and scan the back yard. It looked empty, and I went back inside, shutting the door and leaning against it with my back. By the time Grandma came home, I'd convinced myself that nobody had been there, and that my imagination had been working overtime. It seemed like the only explanation.

*   *   *

The next day, Audrey arrived as usual, but this time she had a pair of scissors in her little knapsack. I'd already washed my hair and sat on a stool in the kitchen. Audrey wrapped a dish towel around my neck. "You're sure you want to do this?" she asked, raising the scissors to the back of my head.

"It's only hair," I said, wondering what I'd gotten myself into. "Make me beautiful, Audrey."

"I'll give it my best shot," she said, and the scissors cut into a chunk of hair. She worked slowly and wouldn't let me see until she was satisfied. My head felt light as the hair fell around me.

At last, Audrey said, "Right. I think that'll do. Now you can look."

I ran into Grandma's bedroom with Audrey right behind me and looked in the mirror over Grandma's dresser. My hair was cut short and funky, and my eyes looked huge with my cheekbones more defined.

"You're a genius!" I shouted and hugged Audrey before she knew what was happening. Her body stiffened at my touch, and she drew away. I quickly dropped my arms to my sides. "I'll visit your shop in Toronto any time," I said, trying to lighten the moment.

Audrey turned to go back into the kitchen. "Yeah, if and when."

"Don't sound so pessimistic. If you want

something badly enough, it'll happen."

Audrey turned towards me, her face shadowed over. "Listen, Jen. I'm still not up to swimming this morning. In fact, I don't think I can come swim with you any more."

"Why not, Audrey? I look forward to seeing you." I stared at her until her eyes lifted to mine. I couldn't begin to read what she was thinking.

"Mom needs me around the house more. She's not doing so well."

"I'm sorry. If you can ever get away later in the day, we could swim at a different time. It doesn't have to be first thing in the morning."

Audrey said, "Don't hold your breath waiting. I probably won't be back any time soon."

She nearly ran out of the cottage, slamming the screen door behind her.

That was the beginning of the end our friendship. It coincided with other disturbing things that reminded me of my first night when I'd thought that someone was watching me in the darkness. It all became intertwined with no real beginning or ending point. If it hadn't been for those mornings in July when Audrey and I had swum and talked together like friends, I wouldn't have questioned what started happening, and things might have ended worse...much worse.

Trouble was the furthest thing from my mind that August afternoon as I guided Grandma's little boat across the lake to Kerry's cottage. Kerry and her mom waved at me and greeted me with shouts of welcome as I neared shore.

Kerry's mom leaned over the water and guided the nose of the boat to the side of their dock. Kerry grabbed the rope and tied the boat so it wouldn't drift away

When I stepped onto dry land, Kerry linked her arm through mine and we started up the path to her cottage. "Have you heard our news?" Her voice was shaking with excitement.

"No. What news?"

"When we arrived last night, we found that somebody'd broken in and stolen some of our things." Kerry's voice was full of drama. "They took some CDs, a couple of bottles of wine, our cribbage board and the silverware. Can you imagine? At first, Mom thought it was just some kids, but I knew it was that Audrey. Remember they said she was stealing where she came from?"

"I can't believe that. Whatever would she need with those things?"

"She just did it 'cause she felt like it. You don't need evidence to know it was her. She has that look about her...you know, like she's bad."

Now I was getting mad. "You're wrong, Kerry. Audrey's not like that, and unless you have proof, I don't want you accusing Audrey. She's my friend."

Kerry dropped my arm and laughed. "You'll see that I'm right. Even my mom says that it was probably Audrey. Anyhow, it's up to the police now." Kerry tossed her head as if that settled things.

I felt sick inside. I knew there were two sides

to Audrey. She didn't let you close to her or invite you to know how she was feeling about pretty near anything. Maybe Audrey was capable of doing what Kerry and her mom thought she'd done, but I didn't want to believe it. I decided to trust Audrey the same way that I'd want to be trusted. It seemed a small enough gift to give a friend.

Six

Another weekend arrived, but this one was definitely a bad weather, stay in the house and read kind of weekend. When I first looked out my bedroom window, the clouds hung black and ominous like big tufts of cotton candy. By the time Grandma had finished her Saturday morning tea, the rain was coming down in torrents, a steady tapping on the roof and windows. The lake was a reflection of grey and gloom. I wasn't feeling very party-like myself.

Grandma was sad too because she couldn't paint in her new wilderness location, but then she decided to make the best of it. We spent the morning baking bread, or rather Grandma baking and me kneading the warm dough. I loved the elastic feel of the risen dough as I worked it and rolled it in and over itself. Grandma formed it into the bread pans, and soon the warm, luscious smell of baking bread hugged every corner of the cottage. Meanwhile, Grandma and I each snuggled under a blanket and played gin rummy. By the end, I owed her six thousand dollars and my first-born child. Luckily, she took an I.O.U.

In the afternoon, the rain let up a bit and we drove to town to buy some groceries. Hawk's Creek has one grocery store, a liquor store, a drug store, a post office and a diner. There's also a small hospital that serves a few other small communities that rim the north shore of Lake Superior and a recreation centre with an outdoor pool. Most locals make the trip to Thunder Bay to buy clothes or anything substantial they might need. They talk about the two-hundred kilometre trip like we in Southern Ontario would talk about a jaunt to the local mall, even though for them, it involves half a day of driving each way. Grandma was over visiting with the butcher, a fellow art connoisseur, discussing oil painting techniques and lamb chops, while I was in the cat food aisle, reading the back of a can that sounded tempting even if meowing wasn't your first language. I was about to put the can back and proceed to critique the contents of a box of canary seed when I heard two local women discussing the break-in at Kerry's cottage.

"I warned Pam Randall that there'd be trouble when that Musquash family moved in. You can always tell by looking at people whether they can be trusted or not."

The woman's friend seemed to agree. "I don't believe in those mixed marriages. The kids always turn out...well odd, you know, not fitting in. It's not that I'm a racist or anything, but that girl stealing from the Randalls just proves what

I'm talking about. They should go back where they came from."

I knocked over three tins of dog food as I dropped my hand. The women became silent, and I heard their carts move down the aisle. I was shaken by their words. I picked up the cans from the floor and went to join Grandma.

She looked at my face and asked, "Are you all right, my dear? You look a bit pale."

I decided there was no point in troubling her. "I'm fine, Grandma. I guess I'm just a bit hungry."

"Well, I know how to fix that." She turned back to the butcher. "Just package up those lamb chops and those sausages, Carl, and we'll be on our way."

We finished our shopping quickly, since there really wasn't too much selection to debate, and left the store with three bags of food. We placed the food in the back of the Jeep before going for milkshakes at the Sprucegrove Diner. We both ordered chocolate malts at the counter and settled ourselves in a booth near the window. Above Grandma's head was a poster advertising a summer dance at the recreation centre the following Tuesday evening.

"Hawk's Creek summer teen dance. Nine o'clock, Tuesday night." I read Grandma the highlights.

"You should go. It'll do you good. You could spend the night with Kerry in town and meet her friends. I worry you're spending too much time alone."

"I'll ask her. It could be fun." I'd been lonely since Audrey had stopped coming over every day.

It might be good to meet some more kids my age.

*   *   *

While Grandma and I were making a dash to the Jeep with the thunder rumbling overhead, I glanced up and saw Mr. Musquash standing under an awning smoking a cigarette. Audrey stood a few feet from him, with her head down and her shoulders slumped. Mr. Musquash looked angry and was pounding the air with one hand as he spoke in Audrey's direction. He looked like a wrestler, stocky and strong with his long mustache bobbing up and down as he talked. Audrey kept nodding, and finally he seemed to relax.

I climbed into the Jeep, and while I was staring out of the window between the raindrops, Jimmy walked outside from a door behind Audrey, looking angry too. I hadn't seen him since he'd brought me home that day from the airport. Even from a distance, he looked good in a denim jacket and blue jeans. His black hair was longer than it had been, almost down to his shoulders. He'd grown a mustache and short beard that looked a lot like stubble. He said something to his dad, and Mr. Musquash looked to be laughing as he patted Audrey on the shoulder. Jimmy lifted his eyes in our direction, and I thought for a second that his bright blue eyes were looking right at me. I looked away, suddenly embarrassed for watching them. I remember thinking that it all seemed very strange. How could Mr. Musquash be so angry one minute and so pleased with Audrey the next? I turned to Grandma for her opinion, but she was looking the other way and missed seeing the Musquashes entirely.

And so Saturday drifted away as did Sunday in a cool, steady rain which lasted until suppertime. I read a novel from Grandma's bookcase called *Cannery Row* by an American author named John Steinbeck and helped Grandma to do the laundry in her little washer and dryer tucked into the back of the kitchen. All in all, we had a good time, singing old camp songs and playing a few more games of rummy in the evenings. I wanted the world to stop and stay like this forever. No worrying about my parents, no worrying about failing school and definitely no worrying about people expecting anything from me.

About eight o'clock Sunday night, the phone rang, and it was Leslie. "Hi, Jen. Ballerina camp ended on Friday, but it got better. I made new friends like you said. Molly is my friend again too, so now I have four friends instead of just one."

"That's great. Where's Mom?" I hadn't spoken to her for a few weeks.

"Mom got called in to work. Mr. Putterman's here with me." Her voice lowered to a whisper. "I wanted to go stay with Dad, but Mom said no. By the way, Dad told me to tell you not to worry about your job, and he hopes you're having a good time. When *are* you coming home, Jen?"

"I don't know yet. I'm not sure I want to come home."

"I hate it when you're gone. Pete came by this week. He seemed sad that you weren't back, and Ambie called twice."

I felt a tug. *Pete came by.* "How did Ambie like camp?"

"She said it was okay. She said she'd learned some computer programming, and it was a blast. Do you think Ambie's getting kind of nutty? Anyhow, she asked what was keeping you up North."

"I'm having a good time. Besides, it's peaceful here with Grandma. I'm going to a dance in town on Tuesday."

"That should be fun. Oh, gotta go, Jen. Mr. Putterman wants to call his office for messages."

"Hugs and kisses, Les. Sorry I can't come home yet."

I noticed that Grandma was watching me over the top of her knitting needles, but she didn't say anything then or later about when I should go home.

*   *   *

Kerry and her mom picked me up Tuesday afternoon to go into town for the dance. Kerry was excited that I was going to sleep over, and she talked non-stop all the way into town until we pulled into their driveway. Then, she said, "Here we are, Jen. The Randall estate!"

Actually, they did have a pretty big house. It was painted a buttery colour and had green shutters. A circular driveway led to a three-car garage. Kerry hopped out of the car and led me into the house and upstairs to her bedroom. She had a canopy bed and white furniture with pink hearts painted all over it. Her window looked out over the front yard. The curtains were also white and ruffled, tied back with sashes. Pictures of Kerry in different beauty contests and dance costumes filled a bulletin board over her desk. Above the bulletin board was a banner that said, "Winning is Everything." Kerry spun around the room and flopped onto her bed. I sat down beside her.

"We're going to meet Mandy Morgan and Leah Pinkett at eight-thirty outside the rec centre. You'll like them. We've been friends since forever," said Kerry.

"Do they ever come up to the lake?"

"Not in July. That's why you've never met them. Mandy spends July in Europe, and Leah has to go to her dad's in New York. You've always gone back to Springhills before August."

It was true. This was the first August I'd spent at Grandma's. I suddenly thought of Ambie. If I were back in Springhills, we'd be hanging out in her bedroom or going to see a movie at the mall. "What do you want to do until it's time to get ready for the dance?" I asked.

"We could play tennis. We have a court out back."

Anything beat sitting around missing Ambie. "That sounds great. I can see if the money my mother shelled out for lessons last summer was worth it."

Kerry laughed. "I have to modestly say that I've had a few lessons myself."

I should have taken that as a big hint and begged off lame. Instead, I survived two hours of Kerry cleaning the court with me as she pounded her serve past my racquet again and again. The few times that I managed to hit the ball back over the net, Kerry thumped it into the farthest corner of the court. She had me running back and forth like a rabbit at a shooting range. Just as I was thinking about collapsing into the asphalt and waiting for some paramedics to carry me off to emergency, Kerry's mom called us for dinner. I would have kissed her if she'd been within reach.

Kerry bounded around the net, having barely broken into a sweat. "Wasn't that fun! You have an interesting serve, Jen."

"Do you think?" I panted.

"You'll have to tell me how you get it to go so slow...and so high."

I tried to smile good-naturedly as she giggled. "It's all in the wrist," I said.

Kerry strode ahead of me and said over her shoulder: "Did I mention I was runner-up in junior tennis provincials two years in a row? I'm hoping to win it this year. I'll show you my trophies after dinner."

"I can't wait," I said.

Seven

We met Mandy and Leah outside the recreation centre around nine o'clock. Both wore identical hip hugger jeans and jean jackets that covered striped green and blue tank tops. I noticed that Kerry was dressed pretty much the same, except the stripes in her tank top were red and white. Mandy was close to six feet tall, with carrot red hair that sprang around her head in big curls. Leah's pixie size and straight black hair were an odd contrast.

Kerry introduced me. "This is my friend Jennifer from the lake."

Leah stared at my black T-shirt before lowering her gaze to my denim skirt. I could tell she thought I was dressed all wrong. "Hi. Kerry told us you come from near Toronto."

"Yes, I'm staying with my grandmother for the summer."

Mandy giggled. "That must be boring. You'll have to come to town more often. Don't you guys just hate hanging out with old people?" She twirled a red curl around and around with her middle finger.

71

Kerry looked at my face and quickly changed the subject. Compared to her friends, she was a study in sensitivity. "Have you seen Michael Burnside yet?"

Mandy answered, "No, but he said he'd be here."

Kerry stuck out her bottom lip, "He'd better be, or he can find himself another girlfriend."

Leah reached up and put her arm over Kerry's shoulders. "Oh, Ker, you know he's got it bad for you. You've got that guy doing whatever you want."

Kerry tossed her streaked blonde hair back and said, "If he knows what's good for him."

Leah had been watching the door. "Let's go inside and see who's here."

We walked into the gym, where the lights had been lowered, except for a spinning globe over the dance floor. People were standing in groups around the walls of the room, and loud dance music was blaring out of the speakers. Nobody was dancing yet. We joined some more of their friends, and soon couples were up dancing while others stood around watching.

A few guys asked me to dance, and before I knew it, the night had flown by. When I finally ran out of partners, I looked around and saw Mandy dancing with a guy half her height. Kerry was clutching onto a clean-cut, preppy-type boy who must have been Michael Burnside. I had no idea what had happened to Leah.

Just then, I saw Audrey. She was draped all

over a big blond guy in a football jacket. They were waltzing to a fast song near the doorway and looked out of place next to all the other couples who were dancing apart. Audrey was wearing tight cutoff shorts and a white tube top. She had her head thrown back and was laughing as if her partner had said something really funny.

I watched for a while and saw them lurching slightly as if they were off-balance. Their movements seemed exaggerated, and I figured they'd been drinking. At last, I saw Audrey break away and head out into the hallway. I nearly ran out of the gym after her. She was disappearing towards the washroom, and I followed her at a distance. She was already in a stall when I entered the washroom, and I stood in front of the mirror, waiting for her to finish. I was still startled by my short hair and was spiking it with my fingers when Audrey appeared behind me.

"Hey, city girl. Sorry I cut your hair?" Her words were softly slurred.

"No, I really like it." I looked at her in the mirror. "How are things going, Audrey?" I could smell the booze coming off her like an overpowering perfume gone bad.

She stared at me in the mirror for a minute before saying, "Just great. Couldn't be better." She turned on the tap and washed her hands.

"I've missed swimming with you."

"Yeah, well. Life is tough." Her mascara was smeared under her eyes in black streaks. Her long black hair looked tangled and hung in clumps. She leaned into the mirror and dabbed at the mascara with a damp paper towel.

I didn't give up. "Maybe, you could come by and we could hang out. We don't need to swim if you don't want to."

She spun around to face me. "Get it through your head, city girl. We've got nothing in common. You and me ain't ever going to be friends, so find some other white girl to cozy up with." Her eyes crackled with anger. "What do I look like? Some kind of pathetic Injun?" She stumbled past me and slammed the door open so that it banged against the wall.

I stood, not saying anything, watching the door swing shut behind her. I guess if I'd had any illusions about being friends with Audrey, that should have about crushed them. It hurt to think that she'd judged me as being so shallow after all the time we'd spent together. I wondered what I'd said or done wrong.

I went slowly into the hallway. I lifted my head and glanced in the direction of the gym. Activity near the main entrance caught my attention. In one of those surreal moments, I stood trance-like, watching Jimmy Musquash throwing some kind of fit. He was waving one fist wildly in the air and holding onto Audrey's arm with his other hand. He was yelling at her so loudly that I could hear him from where I stood.

"How could you be so stupid?" His face was contorted in anger. I wondered how I could ever have thought that he was nice-looking.

Audrey pulled away but then seemed to think better of it. She leaned against him, and Jimmy wrenched her towards the door. The few kids standing nearby watching seemed frozen like they were playing a game of statues.

"You were supposed to stay home. I warned you..." Jimmy yelled as he pulled the door open and dragged her out of the school.

Audrey's leg banged sickeningly against the wall as her feet went out from under her. I heard her say, "Jimmy, stop. Stop, you're hurting me." Then, she was gone, and the door thudded shut.

I felt physically sick but made myself run towards the main entrance. By the time I got there, the three kids who'd been standing around watching were murmuring together and looking upset. I walked past them and pushed open the door. A cool blast of night air hit me in the face, pushing me back a step. My head turned towards squealing tires, and I watched as Jimmy drove his truck full speed out of the parking lot. I glimpsed Audrey sitting hunched as far as possible away from him next to the passenger window. I raised my arm and waved frantically at the receding red tail lights. I was too late to stop them.

*   *   *

Word of the event spread throughout the gymnasium like milk spilled on the dinner table. You could see girls and guys leaning into each other and speaking loudly into each other's ears, trying to make themselves heard above the music. The listeners' faces would form into circles of surprise and excitement. For a small town, this was big news. Families normally went to great lengths to keep their arguments private. Jimmy and Audrey had broken the small-town code.

The dance lost its appeal for me and for several other kids, who started drifting home in small groups. Kerry, Leah, Mandy and I met at the entrance, and we stepped out into the night.

Mandy's red curls bobbed in rhythm to her bouncing steps. She seemed the most excited by the gossip. "I knew that family was bad news. Rosie Johnston saw the whole thing and said Jimmy was cursing Audrey up and down and slapped her right across the face."

"That's not true," I protested. "He never slapped her."

Mandy ignored me. "Audrey was so drunk, she never felt a thing. Rosie said Audrey was laughing at Jimmy and making him mad."

Leah said, "It's her own fault. She's such a disgrace. Did you see the shorts she was wearing? She's such a little tramp."

Kerry chimed in, "What was Tommy Thorton doing with her anyhow? His father better not hear he was with Audrey, or he's in for it. Mr. Thorton is strict."

Mandy and Leah stopped at the turnoff to

their street. Mandy said: "Jimmy sure has his hands full looking after that wild sister of his. Maybe, he needs someone to help him through this time of need." She spun around, pretending to dance with an invisible partner.

Kerry laughed. "You wish. I'll say one thing though. That Jimmy is one hot guy."

Leah backed down the street and held her hands up as if in prayer. "Take me now, Jimmy Musquash. Let me ease your pain!"

Mandy danced alongside her. "Take us both, Jimmy Musquash! We're the hottest girls in Hawk's Creek."

They both doubled over giggling like idiots.

Kerry shook her head in mock despair and said, "You two are big nuts. Everyone knows *I'm* the hottest girl in Hawk's Creek."

I started down the street towards Kerry's house, wishing I'd stayed at the lake with Grandma. Kerry took my arm, "Don't take it so seriously, Jen. It's not worth getting upset about." After a few more steps, she said, "Let's go home and play some video games before bed. We can play for money, if you want."

I looked skyward and said to myself, "Give me strength."

The way my luck was going, there wasn't even a star to wish upon. While we'd been at the dance, a bank of clouds had rolled in, promising a rainy Wednesday. I thought that a good storm would match my mood just fine.

Eight

I got up early and had breakfast with Freddie. He made me sit at the table while he got us bowls of Cocoa Puffs mixed with miniature marshmallows, raisins and milk.

"No bugs or snakes in here?" I asked him before taking my first bite. The spoonful tasted surprisingly good.

He grinned. "Nah. I like you." His red hair was sticking up all over his head in tufts, and he was wearing navy pajamas covered in spacemen.

"Remind me to stay on your good side." I grinned back.

Kerry's mom drove me back to the lake around ten. Kerry was still in bed getting her beauty sleep. She'd rolled over and grunted at me while I collected my stuff. I was just as glad not to have to make small talk. A resolve was taking root in my belly. I wasn't going to listen to any more gossip from Kerry and her friends. I wasn't going to believe the worst of Audrey without proof. I was going to track Audrey down and find out what was really going on.

*   *   *

I waved goodbye to Mrs. Randall and trudged up the path to Grandma's, carrying my knapsack. The rain clouds seemed close and heavy, and the ground was wet from an earlier rain shower. I could smell the earth, warm and rich. I breathed deeply and looked past the cottage to the spruce trees and the grey-blue lake. I was feeling peaceful as I stepped inside and found Grandma in the living room sitting at her easel. I stepped up behind her and looked at her painting. It was nearly finished—a forest scene that didn't look familiar. In the foreground was a turned-over canoe with a black Labrador retriever sitting at attention and looking straight ahead at something we couldn't see. It looked as though it was guarding the canoe or waiting for its master. You could imagine a lot of stories around the picture.

"Grandma, this is beautiful, but I don't think I recognize this place or the dog. Whose is it?"

Grandma turned and smiled at me. "There you are, my darling. Why, this is just a nice place I know of. The dog's name is Blue." She stood and gave me a hug. She smelled of lily of the valley. "How was the dance?"

"Oh, it was okay. I danced quite a bit. I wore the skirt and top you helped me pick out."

"I'll bet. You're a knockout in that denim skirt. The boys were probably lining up."

"I thought about selling tickets."

79

Grandma laughed. "Your mother had the boys lining up too."

It was odd to think of Mom being that popular. It was even odder to think of Mom being my age and dating boys. "Was she much of a dancer?"

"My word, yes. She could really cut a rug."

"What does that mean, cut a rug?"

"An expression that has outlived its time. Your mother was a great dancer. She called last night, by the way."

"She did? What did she say?"

"She agreed that you should stay with me if that's what you want. She's not keen on the idea, but she says she wants you to be happy." Grandma looked at me over her reading glasses.

I felt relieved but sad. After all, this was what I wanted, wasn't it? To stay with Grandma Connelly and never have to be around Mom and her new husband? I pictured Mom back in our house in Springhills. She'd be having her second cup of coffee right about now and had probably already started a load of laundry. Mom was as predictable as they come on her days off. In fact, she was usually pretty predictable in how she reacted to me and Leslie in general. For her to give in this easily meant that she was either relieved to have me out of her hair or she had something else up her sleeve. Was my mother using psychology to outthink me? Maybe, she was trying the "give Jennifer what she wants, then she'll fall back into line" tactic. Lord knows, it had worked before. I had such a wide streak of guilt in my backbone that I always caved when I knew I was giving her trouble.

Grandma said, "Well, you don't have to make any decisions for a few more weeks. I suppose if you're going to spend the year here, we'll have to go into town at the end of the month and sign you up at the school. I don't imagine the Grade Ten class will be too full to accept one more student."

Classes with Kerry, Mandy and Leah. A whole year without Ambie and Pete and Leslie. "Okay, Grandma. I'll think it over," I said.

"I know you will, dear. I have no doubt you'll decide what's best."

*   *   *

It rained for the rest of the day. Grandma painted while I read *Pride and Prejudice.* Jane Austen's writing took a little getting used to, but I quickly became engrossed in the story. After an hour or so, we met for tea beside the potbellied stove. The afternoon shadows had lengthened in the room, so we lit the kerosene lanterns to shake off the gloom.

"Jane Austen knew how to poke fun at people who were stuffy class snobs. I think I'd have liked meeting her," I said.

"Yes, she cut through the nonsense. We could use her to write a book about some of the people in Hawk's Creek." Grandma smiled at me and took out her knitting.

"I'm beginning to think there's a lot of narrow-minded thinkers around these parts." I pretended to have a cowboy drawl.

"Small communities have a way of forming opinions about people that can be hard to shake. Still, little towns have their good points. You can always count on your neighbours to help you through a bad time. Most of 'em step up when necessary."

"Grandma, what do you think about Jimmy and Audrey?" I'd decided not to tell Grandma what had gone on between them at the dance, but I still wanted to hear her impression of their relationship.

She shook her head. "Jimmy has been a help, but he doesn't talk much. I can't say I know all that much about him or his sister. My hunch is that the family isn't a happy one. They keep to themselves for the most part."

"Do you think...that is...could Jimmy be violent?"

"Oh, goodness, I suppose anyone could be violent, given the right set of circumstances. Jimmy behaved well whenever I saw him." Her voice sharpened. "Why do you ask, Jennifer?"

"No reason." I didn't want to get anybody into trouble, so I changed the subject. "When is your exhibition in Thunder Bay?"

Grandma rubbed her forehead. "I meant to tell you this morning. Where has my head gone? The gallery phoned yesterday, and I'll be showing next week. I have to go on Sunday to set up and will be home on the Thursday."

"Are all your paintings finished?"

"Just about. I have this picture to complete, and one other that needs a bit of touching up. I'll have fifteen to show in all."

"You've worked hard, Grandma. It'll be a great show."

"Yes, and I wish you could come too. I think you'd find it extremely dull, though. I also have a day of tests at the hospital. I think it best if you stay here. You could spend the nights with Kerry and her family."

There was that niggling worry again. "Tests for what, Grandma? Aren't you feeling well?"

Grandma laughed. "Oh, I'm just fine, dear. It's only follow-up that my doctor insists I do. Doctors are paid to be worry warts."

"How will you get to Thunder Bay? Driving all that way by yourself will be tiring."

"My good friend, Clara Holmwood, came back from England on the weekend. She dropped by yesterday while you were at Kerry's and said she'd drive me. She has a daughter in Thunder Bay whom she wants to visit. She also has a van that will hold my paintings."

"Well, that's good. You know, Grandma, I'm almost fifteen and going into Grade Ten. I can stay a few nights alone here. I'll be fine."

"Now, I don't know about that. Won't you get lonely all by yourself?"

"Kerry could come here for a couple of days and keep me company. Actually, I like being by myself."

"You won't be able to swim alone."

"No."

"We'll have to think about it a little bit more."

"Okay, Grandma. Just remember, I've been looking after me and Leslie for a few years while Mom worked nights. I'm what you call self-sufficient."

"I can see that, my dear. Well, maybe if Kerry comes to stay and her mom agrees."

"Besides, nothing exciting ever happens in Hawk's Creek," I said.

Famous last words.

*   *   *

Grandma told me that it was one of the wettest Augusts that she could remember. It rained for the next three days, and by the time the sun came out Saturday morning, I was getting cabin fever. I hadn't forgotten the promise that I'd made to myself to find out what was going on with Audrey, and first chance I got, I went in search of her.

I laced on my running shoes, called goodbye to Grandma and started jogging towards the Musquash house. I had to dodge puddles and be careful not to slip on the muddy roads. A wind pushed against me, making it hard to breathe. Still, it sure felt good to be outside.

Finally, the Musquash property came into view. I slowed my pace, stopped at the end of their driveway, scanning the yard and house. Mr. Musquash had finished the front steps, and the new wood stood out in contrast to the rest of the aging house. His saw was still in the yard covered with a piece of plastic, but he wasn't anywhere in sight. In fact, the whole house looked deserted and still. I wasn't going to be put off. I walked determinedly towards the front door and climbed the new steps. The smell of wet fresh-cut cedar filled my nose and I breathed it in deeply. I knocked as loudly as I could and waited. After what felt like a long time, I knocked again. All I heard was the wind whistling through the trees. I jumped off the front steps and circled part way around the back, calling, "Is anybody home? Audrey, where are you?" I couldn't shake the feeling of being watched. It began like a creeping up the back of my neck and made me shiver, even though the sun was warm on my arms and legs. It was the same feeling I'd had twice before, and I gulped back the fear rising in my throat.

A sudden bang made me jump and spin around towards the shed. Its crooked door swung open, then shut on loose hinges. I clutched where my heart was pounding against my ribs and backed away from the house. My eyes darted from window to window, searching for a sign of life. If someone was inside, they remained hidden from my view. Hadn't Audrey said her mom never left the house? "Maybe I've come at a bad time," I whispered to myself and turned away from the house, all the while with that feeling of being watched.

Without looking back, I ran with the wind towards the safety of Grandma's cottage. By the time I started up our driveway, I'd convinced myself that Audrey couldn't have been home and that I'd find her somewhere else when she wanted to be found.

Nine

Saturday morning, I helped Grandma wrap her paintings to take to Thunder Bay. She'd be leaving early the next day, and everything had to be packed and ready.

"You're going to sell all of these, Grandma. They're really beautiful."

"I'll be happy to sell a few of them anyhow. It'll keep me in paints and canvases. It also makes me feel like I'm a real artist. Kind of validates all the time I spend at it to know someone enjoys my work enough to buy it. Have you been doing any art lately, Jennifer? I remember you have a good eye for line and detail."

"No, I haven't done anything all year."

"Well, then. Here's a sketch pad and some pencils that I meant to give you. Why don't you practise a little drawing, and when I come back, we can set you up with an easel and canvas?"

I took the pencils and pad. "Thanks, Grandma. I think I'd like to do some drawing."

"Good." She sat down in her chair. "Well, I think we have them all packaged. I spoke with Mrs. Randall, and she says Kerry will be over later tomorrow to have dinner and spend the night with you. Kerry's really looking forward to the visit. She'll stay over Monday too but has a dental appointment in town on Tuesday. Pam says you can go along and stay with them if you like. I think that might be a good idea."

"Okay. You'll be back Thursday, right?"

"Yes, Clara and I should be back mid-afternoon."

"I'll have supper ready."

"Now, won't that be nice! I have the freezer stocked with food, so help yourself. After I freshen up, we'll drive into town for some bread and milk and fruit to last the week."

"Can I drive as far as the main road?"

"Yes, you can get in some practice."

I threw my arms around her in a quick hug. "You're the best, Grandma."

*   *   *

We came back from town early in the afternoon, and Grandma went to lie down. I'd kept my eyes open for Audrey on our trip but hadn't seen any of the Musquashes. Still, I was certain that I'd thought of a way to find Audrey. I'd remembered that she said she spent her afternoons with Joe, the hermit who lived back in the woods. I'd never actually been to his place, but I remembered Grandma pointing out the dirt path leading to his property about a kilometre away from the main road. I decided to go exploring.

I jogged up the dirt road, past the big rock where I'd first met Audrey. Crickets were singing in the long grass near the road, and I could hear crows cawing in the taller trees. A bee buzzed lazily past my head. The air was warm in the late afternoon sun. After about half an hour of jogging at a steady speed, I saw the path to the hermit's place. It was wide enough for a car or truck to get up, with rutted tire tracks running uphill and into the woods. You had to look closely, though, to find the opening. I was nervous about going into the woods by myself. I remembered the stories Kerry had told me about the old hermit, who had a hunched back and one eye missing. She said that he'd stayed hidden in the woods after his release from prison two summers ago for murdering his wife. I shivered slightly, stepping through the high grass to the path. The stories had to be nonsense, like the ghost stories we told each other with the lights out. I was too old to believe such fantasy, but the knowledge didn't stop me from feeling spooked.

It got cooler as I walked further up the track into the woods. The ground was rutted, and I had to step carefully. There were moss and low bushes growing into the path. When I looked up, I could see the blue sky through the tree branches. Two monarch butterflies flitted in front of me like they were leading the way.

After walking for about fifteen minutes, I stopped to rest for a second, looking up through the branches of a tree. Sprinkles of sunlight landed on my face, and I closed my eyes. Suddenly, I heard something tearing through the bushes. I opened my eyes and saw a dark shape lunge out of the underbrush towards me. I jumped back a step and stood frozen in place, too scared to move or scream. A huge black Labrador retriever stood a few feet from me, growling deep in his throat. His fur was standing up on his neck, and he looked ready to attack.

I swallowed hard and kept as still as I could. I could hear something else coming through the underbrush behind the dog. Suddenly, a man appeared. He was wearing a black baseball cap and a red and blue checkered shirt. In his hands was a rifle. He held it with two hands across his chest, pointing the barrel at the sky. He stood for what seemed like a long time looking at me.

Then he said, "I wondered when we'd meet, Jennifer."

I squeaked, "How do you know my name?"

He smiled, and his eyes seemed kind. "I'm friends with your grandma. She's been asking me to come by and see you. I'm not much at meeting new people, though."

The dog relaxed at the sound of its master's voice.

"Is this Blue?" I asked.

"Yes, I guess your grandma showed you her painting, did she? I'm Joe." He took one hand off his rifle and reached out to shake my hand.

As I stepped towards him, Blue growled. I dropped my hand.

"Blue! Enough!"

Blue turned and looked at Joe.

"Reach down your hand with your palm up, and let Blue smell it. He'll be friends with you soon enough."

I was reluctant to lower my hand anywhere near Blue's teeth, but I did as I was told. Blue's tail began to wag as he sniffed my hand. I felt his sandpapery, wet tongue on my fingers. "He's a beautiful dog."

"Thanks. I like to think so. Would you like to have a cold drink before you head back?"

I realized that Grandma'd been visiting Joe's place to paint Blue. If she and Audrey felt comfortable with him, then it must be all right to accept a drink. "Yes, that'd be great. Does Audrey Musquash happen to be here too?"

Joe led me through the brush. He said gruffly, "Audrey hasn't been here for a few weeks now. I've missed her company."

His cabin was tiny, but it had a front screened-in porch with two rocking chairs. Joe sat me in one and went inside to get us a drink. I noticed birdhouses and birdfeeders high up on the trees in front of the cabin. Blue padded behind Joe and lay down at his feet after he served me a glass of pink lemonade.

"Do you like living here alone?" I asked. "It's really peaceful," I added.

"I guess I'm just used to it. Yeah, I like it fine."

"I've never seen you in town. How do you get your groceries?"

Joe rubbed his white beard. His eyes were chocolate brown and gentle on close inspection. "Claude Greenspon leaves me food at the end of the road on Tuesdays at a time we've agreed on. I also have a garden out back, and I hunt for partridge or rabbits. That's what I was doing when I came across you."

I didn't like to ask anything more personal, and Joe didn't offer anything more about himself. We rocked in friendly silence while I finished my lemonade. I set my glass down and stood to go. Blue stood too, his tail wagging against Joe's leg.

I said, "If Audrey comes to see you, would you tell her I'm looking for her?"

Joe nodded. "Say hi to your grandma. I hope her show goes well in the city."

"I do too. She's pretty excited."

"Blue will walk back with you to the road. Now that he knows you, he'll be looking forward to you coming again."

"Thanks for the lemonade, Joe." I bent and scratched behind Blue's ears. "I'm glad we finally met."

"Next time, I'll get you started building a bird feeder, if you like." He smiled shyly.

"That would be great."

Blue led me down the path and turned back just before we came to the road. I hadn't found Audrey, but I'd made two new friends, and that made the day worthwhile.

Ten

After supper, Grandma said, "How about a boat ride around the lake? I always miss being here when I'm away, so a boat tour will keep Hawk's Creek fresh in my memory."

"Sure, Grandma. I'll get the life jackets."

She let me steer the boat, and we headed across the lake, and around the western part of the shoreline. After we'd made our way to the farthest point, I turned the bow back towards our cottage. As our dock came into view, Grandma reached over and tapped my arm. She yelled over the motor, "Let's stop here and watch the sun start to set. We're close enough to home that we can dock before it gets dark."

So we sat quietly, listening to the water lap against the side of the boat and the loon calling wild echoing sounds across the lake. The sun was setting in a blaze of reds and oranges.

I sighed. "Grandma, how could anybody want to be anywhere other than Hawk's Creek?"

Grandma smiled at me. "It's a bit of heaven on earth all right."

After a while, I said, "I met Joe today. He's very nice."

A look of surprise crossed Grandma's face, but then she nodded. "Yes, he's one fine man." She didn't ask me what I'd been doing that far into the woods.

"Joe said that you were friends. I recognized Blue from your painting."

"Yes, Joe and I spent a lot of time together this past winter. I've grown very fond of him."

I knew Grandma was telling me something more. "Is he your boyfriend, Grandma?" I said teasingly.

"Well...one might say. We're good company for each other. We're at ease when we're together."

I was happy to know Grandma had someone. "Why's he so reclusive and shy? He doesn't even go into town for groceries."

Grandma's face turned serious in the fading sunlight. "His wife, daughter and grandchild were killed in a car accident about five years ago. Since then, he spent some time in the hospital but moved here a few years ago. His family used to come to Hawk's Creek when he was a boy, so he came back to find some peace, I suppose. The accident broke his spirit for a bit, but Hawk's Creek has been a good tonic."

"Well, I like him, Grandma. He's offered to let me build a birdhouse."

"He's quite a carpenter. He built that cottage and all the furniture." Grandma looked towards the dock. "It's time to head in now, dear. We don't want to be caught out here in the darkness."

*   *   *

The next day, Grandma left early for Thunder Bay. I got up and saw her off, then went back to bed. I woke up again, because the phone was ringing in the kitchen. I leaped out of bed and picked up the receiver on the fifth ring.

Leslie's voice hummed in my ear, "Jen, what took you so long to answer?"

"I was sleeping." I yawned loudly.

"Mom is sleeping too. She's on nights."

I knew what that meant. Leslie had to stay quiet and look after herself until mid-afternoon. Mom also got crankier as her night shifts went along. "How're things with you, Les?" I asked.

"Good. Mom let Dad take me for the weekend. I helped in his garage on Saturday and then we went for pizza. He brought me home this morning, but we're going to see a movie after lunch."

"I wish I could be there too."

"Do you, Jen? Are you coming home soon?"

"No. I might stay here and go to school. Grandma said I could."

Leslie was quiet. I could hear the soft in and out of her breathing.

"You know I don't want to live with Mom and Putterman. Staying here looks like my only alternative," I said, trying to make her understand.

"Maybe I could come live with you too." Her voice sounded hopeful.

"Mom would never let you go."

"I could ask. She might want to be alone with Mr. Putterman when they get married."

"He likes having you there, Les. Besides, Mom wouldn't marry him if he didn't like kids."

"I could tell Mom he doesn't like me. Maybe she won't marry him then."

I laughed, "The problem is, he does like you. Anyone can see that."

"Stupid Mr. Putterman."

"Stupid Dad. How did he get us into this mess?"

Leslie sighed. "Mom sure is mad at him. She only let me stay with him this weekend because Mr. Putterman is away on a conference."

"How is Dad?"

"We had fun yesterday. He misses you too."

"Well, say hi for me."

"I will, and Jen?"

"Yeah?"

"I asked Dad for a cat to keep at his place, and guess what?"

"What?"

"He's thinking about it! I'm going to call it Pooky."

I could suddenly see Leslie's eyes shining and her pixie hair cut bobbing up and down in excitement. I tried to sound happy. "That's great, kid. You keep working on him."

"I will. Bye, Jen."

"Bye, Les."

I listened to the dial tone long after she'd clunked down the receiver. I almost felt a tear slide out of the corner of my eye. Almost, except I blinked it away.

*   *   *

Kerry came before supper and stayed for two nights. Nothing exciting happened. The days were sunny and warm, and we swam a few times a day and suntanned. We also ate everything in sight, so it felt good to jog in the mornings while Kerry was still asleep. Every morning, I went by Audrey's place, but I never saw anyone in the yard. I was too timid to repeat my trip to the Musquashes' front door.

Kerry seemed a little subdued the second afternoon as we sat side by side in the hammock. Before I could ask her what was wrong, she started talking. Sometimes, Kerry rambled from one subject to another without breaks in between, and I had to pay close attention in case she popped a question at me. "You have it so good here, Jennifer. No little brat of a brother or parents breathing down your back. It's like nobody in my family ever heard of the word privacy. The police never did prove that Audrey stole our stuff, by the way, and we thought it was pretty nervy that she denied breaking in. I'm glad you're not hanging out with her any more. Leah Pinkett says she likes your hair. She's thinking about getting hers cut."

I took advantage of Kerry's need to breathe and jumped in. "Well, maybe, you were wrong about Audrey. It's not a good idea to form opinions about someone without knowing them." This time, I would stand up for my friend, because I still thought of her that way.

"Oh, Jennifer. You say the *cutest* things. Next you'll be telling me that there's nothing biologically wrong with my little toad of a brother." Kerry laughed and began rocking the hammock backwards and forwards. Her mood had lightened considerably, while mine had gotten worse when I remembered that I hadn't been able to find Audrey to ask her what was going on with her and Jimmy. Maybe I wasn't such a good friend after all.

Tuesday morning at around ten o'clock, Mrs. Randall came to pick up Kerry for her dental appointment in town. "Jennifer, would you like to come with us? Kerry wants to do some school clothes shopping before we come back to the lake."

"Thank you, Mrs. Randall, but I don't feel like shopping. Why don't you both go, and I'll stay here? I'm reading a good book, and I don't mind being alone for the day."

"Well...if you're sure. I suppose it will be okay if I drive Kerry back after supper."

I waved until they were out of sight. I'd forgotten how much Kerry liked to talk. She didn't seem to care if I was listening or not. An afternoon alone without her chatter in my ear was stretching before me like a welcome friend.

Storm clouds gathered all day. By suppertime, ripples of thunder rumbled off to the east. Soon, fork lightning zagged across the sky, coming closer and closer until the storm was directly overhead and the rain started streaking the windows and pattering on the roof. I closed all the windows, noticing that the wind had come up and was beating rain onto the kitchen floor. To keep out the gloom, I lit the kerosene lanterns in the living room and started a fire in the potbellied stove. Soon the room was warm and cosy, although I could hear the wind howling around the house like an angry guest trying to get inside.

I was just sitting down near the stove with a supper of chili that I'd defrosted from the freezer when the phone rang, making me jump and spill milk onto my lap. I ran into the kitchen, dabbing at my pants with a paper towel as I grabbed the phone.

The line was crinkly with static. "Jennifer, is that you?" Mrs. Randall's voice came faintly across the wire.

"Yes, I'm here!" I yelled so she could hear me.

"Good, dear. I'm afraid we got delayed in town. Someone stole the van, and we had to wait for the police to drive us back to the lake."

"Oh no! Did they find out who did it?" I felt a sinking feeling. Audrey was sure to be blamed.

"No, they're looking at a few leads. Anyway, Jennifer, with this storm, it's not safe to come get you by boat. Will you be okay there overnight alone?"

"I'll be fine. Don't worry about me."

The line was getting cracklier. "We'll come across in the morning, first thing when the storm ends. Lock the..."

The phone was suddenly dead. The overhead light in the kitchen flickered and went out as well. This was beginning to feel like an evening out of a horror movie.

"Don't be such a baby," I told myself, but that didn't stop me from rushing around the cabin to lock all the doors and windows. I was out of breath when I finally sat down in my grandmother's chair to eat my cold chili. I decided to read the rest of my book by lamplight and go to bed early. With any luck, I'd sleep through the worst, and the storm would be over when I woke up.

Eleven

I jolted awake to find myself still sitting in my grandmother's chair with my book in my lap. I looked at the mantle clock ticking above the bookcase and realized that I'd been dozing for a few hours. It was now nearly ten-thirty. I rubbed my eyes and stretched like a cat, trying to get the blood flowing again. Then, I padded over to the back door to peer outside into the inky blackness. The rain had lessened, but the wind was still howling around the cabin like a banshee. I wasn't quite sure what a banshee was, but it seemed like a good word to describe the gusts of wind that rattled the windows and roared down the chimney.

I turned back towards my bedroom, thinking about getting into my pajamas and pulling the quilt over my head. The cottage seemed to rock in the wind, and I wanted to be somewhere that felt snug and safe. I opened the bedroom closet and reached for the fleecy green pyjamas, the ones covered in panda bears that looked perfect for such a stormy night. Without warning, a wild knocking started at the back door. It was so unexpected that I screamed as you do when somebody sneaks up on you. Then I stood perfectly still, clutching my hands together against my mouth with my heart pounding so hard, I thought it would come out of my chest. Still, the knocking went on and on. I edged my way to the bedroom door and out into the kitchen. The knocking stopped as quickly as it had begun. I watched in terror as the doorknob slowly turned as if a ghost were playing with the handle. My frantic race to lock all the doors and windows didn't seem so silly now. I watched, frozen, as the knob turned back into place. Almost instantly, the fierce knocking started again.

I plucked up the courage to creep towards the door. I was just a few feet from it when the knocking stopped abruptly for the second time. I leaned closer and heard something slide heavily down the outside of the door. I crouched to the floor and thought I heard sobbing coming from just outside. It sounded half-animal and half-human. The flesh on my arms was covered in goose bumps, and I was breathing in quick, noisy gasps.

My voice came out shaky and high-pitched. "Who's there?" I tried again, this time louder, making my voice harsher. "Who are you? Go away or I'll call the police!" My threat seemed feeble, especially since I knew the phone was dead, and that even if it had been working, I could have been murdered thirty times over before a police car could make it from town.

Her scream came clearly through the door. "Jennifer! City girl! Let me in!"

"Audrey!" I grabbed the door handle and turned the lock, swinging the door open in a whoosh. She toppled onto the floor, her wet black hair hanging in her face and her clothes forming a puddle on the kitchen floor.

"Audrey, what are you doing out in this storm?" I asked in disbelief, grabbing her by the arm and helping to pull her to her feet.

She stood unsteadily and leaned against me for a second before straightening herself. "Lock the door! Lock the door! He might be coming to get me!" She pushed the hair out of her face and then I saw.

"Audrey, your face! It's all black and blue! Oh my God—you're hurt!"

Audrey stumbled to a chair, and I quickly turned the deadbolt. Was someone out there watching the cottage from the darkness? I shivered and turned back towards Audrey.

"Let me get some ice for your face." I ran to the freezer and grabbed an ice pack. The fridge was still cold, even though the power had been off a while, but it wouldn't be long before food in the freezer started melting. I hoped the power would be back on soon. I wrapped the ice pack in a tea towel and knelt beside Audrey, gently pressing it against her right eye and cheek.

She took it from me. "Thanks. Is the door locked?" Her voice hummed with fear.

"Yes. Nobody can get in. You're safe here." I

touched her arm. "Audrey, you're soaked. I'm going to get you some dry clothes. Do you want to come sit by the stove in the living room?"

She nodded, and I led her to Grandma's chair. I found some dry sweatpants, underwear, socks and a big sweatshirt in my room and brought them to Audrey.

"Thanks. Could you turn around while I change?" Her hands were trembling on the clothes resting in her lap.

"Sure." With my back to Audrey, I said, "This isn't right, Audrey. Jimmy can't get away with this."

She was silent for a moment. Finally, she whispered his name, as if defeated. "Jimmy."

"Yes. I saw how he dragged you out of the school dance. You don't have to take this from him." I tried to make my voice strong.

"You don't understand. Nobody understands."

I turned as she pulled the sweatshirt over her head. I could see yellowing bruises on her stomach and on the underside of her arms. Some bruises looked newer, still dark and angry. "Oh, Audrey! You have to let me help you."

"The last person who tried to help me got arrested."

"What do you mean?"

"He fixed it so my teacher got set up for trying to rape me. He made me go along with it." Audrey's head bowed against her chest. "Every time I make friends, he ruins it. I shouldn't drag you into this."

"No, Audrey. We're friends, and I'm going to help you. You can stay here tonight, and we'll go to the police in the morning. Are you in any pain?"

She shook her head. "I'm so tired, Jennifer. I just want to sleep." Her face shut down, and I knew she didn't want to talk about it any more.

"You can have my bed, and I'll sleep in my grandmother's room."

"Okay," she nodded, and I showed her the bathroom and my bed. She walked as if she were sleepwalking and climbed heavily into bed.

I pulled the covers up over her and whispered, "I'm just in the next room. Sleep well, Audrey. Try not to think about anything until morning. We'll figure something out then."

She grunted in response and rolled towards the wall.

I took the kerosene lamp and my pajamas and went into Grandma's room. I missed her so much at that moment that I almost sobbed. After I'd climbed into bed with the covers up around my head, I lay a long time listening to the wind and the rain pounding on the roof and against the window. I kept my ears wide open for any sounds of someone trying to get into the cottage. When I finally fell asleep, I still kept jolting awake to check the room and to listen to the night sounds. The last time I remembered looking at the clock, it was three a.m. I closed my eyes a final time with images of Jimmy dragging Audrey out of the dance, her legs and arms flailing, and Jimmy's face mean and angry. In a sudden dream leap, Audrey and Jimmy were running around Grandma's cottage, laughing and calling at me to come play while I watched from the dock. I couldn't make my legs move to join them, but soon the images slipped away, and I fell into a deeper sleep that lasted until morning.

Twelve

When I opened my eyes, the sunlight was streaming into my bedroom, and I could hear Audrey moving around in the next room. I heard her go into the bathroom and run the water, then flush the toilet. I got up quickly and pulled on my clothes from the day before. When she came out of the bathroom, I was sitting at the kitchen table waiting for her. She didn't notice me at first, and her face looked sad. Her right eye was ringed in black and purple, and her cheek was swollen. She grimaced as she walked, but when she saw me, her face went still and expressionless.

"Morning, city girl. Looks like the storm stopped."

"Good morning, Audrey." It was strange how we could say all the normal things you say in the morning, as if nothing had happened the night before. "Would you like a glass of orange juice?"

"Yeah, that'd be nice. Then I have to get home."

I nearly gasped. "Do you think that's a good idea? It might not be safe."

Audrey's eyes looked empty. She said, "It'll be fine now. He'll be sleeping it off."

"Well, I'm coming with you."

Audrey shook her head, "No, I'll be fine. I just overreacted last night. Really, I always make things seem worse than they are. It's one of my least pleasing personality traits." She attempted a smile.

"Well, I'm coming with you anyway." I could see that Audrey didn't have the strength to fight me.

I convinced her to have a bowl of corn flakes with her orange juice, then we set out together down the road towards her house. The morning had cooled off, but every so often the sun slipped out from behind the cloud cover and warmed us in its blinding light.

"It looks like it'll be a better day today," I said. "I believe the storm has moved on."

We trudged further. It was slow going for Audrey, and I matched my steps to hers.

She stopped and faced me. "Jennifer, I don't want you to talk about what happened last night. I don't want you to tell anybody, not even your grandma. Do you promise?" Her dark eyes stared into mine, intense and pleading.

"How can I promise that, Audrey? I can't let him do this to you."

"You have to. Talking about it won't do any good."

"Why don't you leave?"

"Ha. I've tried that. I never get too far. And besides, I have to look after Marilyn and Doris."

Suddenly, she looked anxious. "I never should have left them last night. Jimmy's going to be mad."

"As if you should care what *he* thinks."

We were nearly to her driveway when we saw her father walking towards us. He wore a red hunting jacket and carried a walking stick. His eyes darted back and forth between me and Audrey, but as we got closer he looked at me and smiled. Still, his eyes didn't look happy. I noticed that his clothes were rumpled, as if he'd slept in them. As we got really close, I could smell stale alcohol coming off him, and I looked at Audrey, who stood stock still beside me. She was watching him like someone would watch a poisonous snake. I had a sudden thought. *Oh my God, could it be her dad?*

"There you are, Audrey. We wondered where you'd gotten to last night. You should have told us you were sleeping over with...Jennifer, isn't it?" He grinned at me as if we were friends.

"Sorry, Dad." She kept her head down so that her hair hid her face.

I turned to her. "Can I have a glass of water before I head back? I'm awfully thirsty."

Mr. Musquash answered for her, "Of course you can. Audrey, you go and get your friend some water, and we'll wait outside." He motioned for Audrey to go into the house.

I had to think of some way to stay longer until I could figure out how to help Audrey. I scanned the windows, trying to see if anybody else was home. "Is Jimmy here?"

"No. He got held up by the storm last night, I guess."

With a sickening lurch in my stomach, I looked at Mr. Musquash. He'd just confirmed the idea that had been running around in my mind. Jimmy hadn't hurt Audrey last night. He hadn't been home.

Mr. Musquash looked at me and saw something in my face that made him say, "You look like you've seen a ghost." His voice lowered and he leaned towards me, holding his walking stick with both hands. "It's nice Audrey has a friend like you. Maybe, you can convince her to stay away from that boyfriend of hers. Her mother and I are very concerned that he's been hitting her. We're thinking about pressing charges."

"What boyfriend?" I asked, not believing him for a minute.

"Why, Tommy Thorton, of course."

Tommy Thorton. The blond boy I'd seen her slow dancing with. Had I jumped to the wrong conclusion about Audrey's dad? I looked at him standing in front of me and smelled the alcohol and cigarette smoke that seemed to be leaking out of his skin. He was smiling at me as if we were sharing a secret, but his eyes looked cunning. I remembered Audrey telling me, *He fixed it so my teacher got set up for trying to rape me. He made me go along with it. Every time I make friends, he ruins it.* Audrey didn't know

Tommy Thorton in their last town. Who else besides her father and Jimmy had the power to make her lie about a teacher? Who was trying to blame someone else for the bruises that covered Audrey's poor body?

I said, "Tommy Thorton doesn't seem like that kind of person."

"You never can tell these things, sweetheart. Don't be fooled. We've done everything we can to keep him away from Audrey. Now, it might be time to bring in the police." He seemed suddenly eager for me to leave. "I think you'd better head home now. We have things to deal with here."

"But, I..."

"I said, *go home.* Audrey'll call you later." He turned towards the house as if I was excused.

I stood for a second, thinking about what I should do. I didn't just want to leave Audrey, but I was scared to stand up to Mr. Musquash.

Just then, the front door swung open and Audrey pushed her way out, dragging Marilyn and Doris by the hands, one on each side of her. The door banged shut behind them. Audrey marched towards us with the two little girls desperately trying to hide behind her.

As they got closer, I caught sight of Marilyn, the eight-year-old, peeking from behind Audrey's back. I looked in horror at the blackening bruise on the side of her face. Her right eye was nearly swollen shut.

Audrey's face was a mixture of fear and

hatred. She screamed at her father, "How could you do this? How could you hit Marilyn?" Tears were seeping out of Marilyn's good eye.

Doris kept her head bowed, but I could hear her whimpering.

"Audrey! I didn't hit her. She fell against the door last night. If you hadn't gone out, it wouldn't have happened." The last words came out whiny and self-righteous.

Audrey screamed louder. "Don't lay this on me! I'm leaving, and I'm taking them with me. This time, I'm telling Jimmy how bad it's gotten." She stomped past us, pulling her sisters along behind her.

Mr. Musquash leaped after her and grabbed her by the arm. He screamed, "You're not taking them away from here. They're mine! You useless piece of trash."

Audrey released Marilyn and Doris. They stepped back and huddled together, watching Audrey struggle with their father. Audrey tried to pull away from him, while he shook her back and forth by the arm. He raised his walking stick as if he was getting ready to swing it at her.

I jumped forward and grabbed the stick. Mr. Musquash shoved Audrey away and yanked the stick from my hands. He pulled it back and whacked it across my shoulder so fast that I didn't have time to react. It hit me with a crack, and I felt pain across my shoulder and arm.

"Stay out of this," Mr. Musquash growled at me. He reeled around and pointed the stick in

Audrey's direction. "You leave this place now and never come back. I'm through with you. Your sisters are staying with me."

A noise from the front steps made us all turn towards the house. The Musquashes stood as if in a trance, seeing something they'd not thought possible. While they'd been arguing, Mrs. Musquash had stepped outside onto the front step. I remembered Audrey telling me that her mother hadn't left the house for two years. I looked at Mrs. Musquash's face. Her frightened eyes seemed to be looking for somewhere to hide. She was dressed in a flowered housecoat, and her hair was pulled back in a long braid. Her shoulders hunched forward, and I worried that she might fall.

Mr. Musquash took a step towards her, his hands stretched forward.

Her voice wavered. "Ed, that's enough."

"Audrey's being difficult again. I've told her to leave." His voice was harsh.

A look passed between them before Mrs. Musquash raised her eyes to stare over his head.

"I've called Jimmy, and he's bringing the police. You put that stick down and go have a rest until they get here." Her voice trembled, and her legs were shaking.

We stood afraid to move, waiting to see what Mr. Musquash would do next. He looked at his wife for a moment more before whining, "Connie, you shouldn't have called the police. If anyone says anything, it'll go bad."

I was holding onto my shoulder with my good hand. My arm was hanging at an odd angle and hurt to move. I looked past Mr. Musquash and saw Jimmy's black truck barrelling up the road towards the house. The truck grew in size as he got closer until I could hear his truck tires thumping up the driveway. The others heard them too and turned their eyes toward the road. Jimmy stopped his truck a few metres from us and jumped out. He ran towards us until he was standing in front of Audrey, facing his father.

"Put the stick down, old man."

"Jimmy, it's not how it looks."

Jimmy looked at Marilyn's swollen face and at Audrey's bruised cheek and black eye. Then his flashing blue eyes swept over his mother leaning against the railing on the front steps and settled on my arm hanging oddly at my side. "You told me this had stopped. This was your last chance." Jimmy's hands were fists at his sides.

Mr. Musquash tried to stare down Jimmy. Finally, he threw down the stick and pushed past everyone into the house. He said, "I'm going to lie down. I'm sick of you people. You're nothing but garbage. The whole lot of you can go to hell." The front door slammed behind him.

We all stood still for a moment, trying to take in what had just happened. It was a lot of ugliness packed into such a short time. Then Doris started crying in big wailing sobs. I felt a wave of nausea as I tried to move my shoulder. Jimmy crossed the yard and reached for me. "Come sit on the steps. You look like you're ready to pass out." He put his arm around my waist and led me to the stairs.

Audrey ran to her mother. Marilyn and Doris also bolted up the stairs and wrapped their bodies around their mother's waist. Mrs. Musquash patted Doris's head and kept saying over and over, "Hush, child. Everything is all right now."

Jimmy looked up at his mom and said, "The time has come for us to tell the truth, okay, Ma?"

We all looked at Mrs. Musquash.

She nodded her head wearily and said, "Yes, no more excuses." She put her hand under Audrey's chin and kissed her on the cheek as a police car started up the driveway to the Musquash house.

Thirteen

For the next week, I met Audrey on the dock every night after supper. We'd sit with our feet resting in the cool water, sometimes talking and sometimes just listening to the rhythm of the waves against the shore and the loon calling its haunting song. My arm was in a sling, and the doctor had said that my collar bone would take six weeks or so to heal. It ached a bit, but I was getting used to it.

One evening, Audrey said, "I'm not really his daughter, you know. Mom and Dad broke up after Jimmy was born, and Mom started seeing someone else. I guess she went back to live with Dad but kept seeing the other man. When I was born, Mom and Dad got into a fight, and she told him that I wasn't his kid. Dad never ever forgave her...or me. As I got older, he got meaner, especially when he drank. When Jimmy went away earlier this summer, it got pretty bad."

I put my good arm around her shoulders, "He can't hurt you any more."

"After he hit me, he always said if I told anyone, I'd live to regret it."

"That's what people like him say to keep you quiet. Once you tell, they get in a lot of trouble."

"It seems so easy now, but I was scared to tell. He had a way of making me look bad. Then, I just started believing I was." She shrugged. "Even you thought it was Jimmy."

"Why did Jimmy drag you out of the dance like that?"

"Dad sent him to get me. He made up some story about me and Tommy Thorton that got Jimmy mad. Plus, I was supposed to be looking after Doris and Marilyn."

"Still, Jimmy didn't need to drag you out like that."

"He was getting frustrated. He'd tried to leave for the summer but came back because I'd begged him to. He knew Dad was mean, but I'd never told him that Dad was hitting me. Dad normally only hit me where you couldn't see the bruises. Jimmy told me that he couldn't put his finger on what was wrong, but he felt he had to come home to keep a lid on things." Audrey laughed bitterly. "He thought I was turning into a wild girl—between him and Dad, I wasn't allowed to do much."

"Your dad has big problems."

"The funny thing is, he wasn't mean all the time. He was usually nice to me the next day after he hit me. He said he never meant to."

"How's your mom doing?"

"Better. She sits outside now, and once she walked to the road and back. Jimmy says he's going to take her for a ride in his truck when she's up to it."

"I'm glad, Audrey."

"Me too, city girl."

* * *

Grandma had come home that Thursday excited about her show. She'd sold four pieces and felt on top of the world. I still remember her face when she saw my arm in the sling. I tried to reassure her that nothing much had happened.

She said, "Oh Jennifer, I can't forgive myself for leaving you alone. What if something worse had happened?"

"Well, nothing worse did happen, and maybe this is all for the best anyway," I said. "Mr. Musquash kind of got cornered into telling the truth."

Grandma said, "Well, I suppose something good did come out of this. I'd rather you hadn't been involved, though."

"All's well that ends well," I answered.

Grandma smiled at me. "You're one good kid, you know that, Jennifer?"

I smiled back, "As long as you think so, Grandma."

* * *

I still hadn't decided about going back to Springhills. School was starting next week, and

I knew I had to make up my mind soon. That morning, I went for a walk to visit Joe. I'd started going every other day to see him. He always made mint tea while I played with Blue.

"Grandma thinks we should have an 'end of the summer' party Friday night. You know, a barbecue. Grandma's promised to make cherry pies. I was hoping you'd come."

Joe set the steaming mug of tea beside me on the table. "I suppose that would be an event I couldn't miss. Will anyone else be there?"

"Grandma's going to ask Audrey and her family and Mrs. Randall and Kerry and Freddie."

"You can count me and Blue in. It might be time we got back in the social swing."

"I'll make sure we get some special dog biscuits. Would you like that, Blue?" I asked, scratching behind his ears. His tail thumped up and down on the floor.

I stayed for about an hour, then walked the trail to the road. It was a warm summer day. The sunshine filtered through the spruce trees from a satin blue sky. I walked home slowly, enjoying the solitude and the birds chirping from the woods. I began jogging as I neared Grandma's cottage. I was surprised to see a cream-coloured van in her driveway, since we weren't expecting anyone. It was a van I didn't recognize. I walked up the path to the cottage and pushed open the back screen door. Then, I stopped with my mouth open.

"Surprise, Jen! Surprise!" Leslie jumped

across the kitchen and threw her arms around my stomach.

"Leslie!" I yelled, hugging her with my good arm. "Dad, you're here too!"

"We figured if the mountain wouldn't come to us, we'd have to come to the mountain," Dad laughed, coming over to give me a hug too. He was dressed in khaki shorts and sandals and looked more relaxed than I remembered him being in Springhills

"Well, this is about the nicest surprise I could have asked for," I said and meant it.

Dad held me at arm's length. "I think you've grown about an inch, not to mention the arm sling fashion statement you've got going on."

"That'll be off in a few more weeks." I saw Grandma shake her head. "Okay, another month. It doesn't hurt any more, though."

Dad said, "That's good. Your grandmother was just filling me in on your adventure."

"We thought it better not to worry you." I looked at Grandma again, "Okay, I didn't want to worry you." I figured I'd better change the subject. "Dad, you're looking pretty cool with your new haircut. You've got a spiky look happening there."

"I could say the same for you." He reached over and mussed up my hair, and I thought about the day Audrey had come over to cut it. That day seemed like a long time ago.

Leslie jumped up and down in front of me. "Can we go swimming now, Dad?"

"Sounds like a plan. Then I'll barbecue the salmon and potatoes we brought from town, and Grandma and Jen can tell us all about their summer in Hawk's Creek."

"Oh, you know, Dad," I said, "nothing much ever happens in Hawk's Creek."

Grandma smiled at me and said, "I'll just make a lemon meringue pie while you're down at the water. This is a cause for celebration. Yes, indeed, this is turning into one fine day."

Fourteen

Thursday passed in lazy happiness, then it was the day of the party. The morning dawned sunny and warm. Still, it was the kind of sunshine that wasn't as strong as on a July morning, and I knew autumn was waiting in the wings. Leslie, Dad and I drove to town to buy the food and drinks for the party while Grandma baked her famous cherry pies.

As we were loading up the van, I said to Dad, "Can we get Grandma something special?"

"What did you have in mind?"

"I was thinking a wool throw rug for her chair in the living room. She says it gets chilly on winter nights."

"Great idea. Did I also tell you that we have an appointment at Lloyd's Photographic Studio in fifteen minutes?"

"Is that why you made me have a shower this morning, Dad?" asked Leslie.

Dad laughed. "Guilty as charged. I want a nice framed photo of you and Jennifer to give to Grandma. I also want a copy for me and one for your mom. You guys are growing up way too fast. We need a few memories."

Leslie said, "We could get you and Mom one picture if you lived together."

Dad stopped and looked at Leslie for a moment before answering. His voice sounded sad. "Ah, Leslie, you've got to accept that's not the way things are."

I tried to lighten the moment. I took Leslie by the arm and said, "You can never have too many pictures of our modest selves. We're the two hottest-looking chicks alive. Bring on the lucky photographer."

Leslie giggled. "You're so kooky, Jennifer."

Dad laughed too. He said, "Yes, that photographer doesn't know just how privileged he is."

I said, "Well, we'll try not to break his camera, anyway."

*　　*　　*

After we finished up in town, we headed back to Grandma's to set up for the party. We put deck chairs in a semicircle near the dock and laid a table with wild flowers and dishes. Dad filled a metal tub with ice and drinks. Leslie and I made the potato salad. Then we waited.

Around two thirty, Mr. and Mrs. Randall and Kerry and Freddie arrived by boat from their cottage. Freddie and Leslie circled each other for five minutes, before Freddie finally said, "I caught a frog and named it Kerry. It's in a bucket at our cottage. Do you want to go dig up some worms? We can call them Kerry too."

Leslie giggled, and they picked up shovels and pails, and headed down the shore. Kerry and I sat in the deck chairs. She stuck out her tongue at Freddie's back.

I smiled and asked, "Did you get your van back?"

"Yes, the police found it abandoned on a dirt road the other side of Hawk's Creek. They think someone was joyriding."

"You sound like you're not sure."

"Well, I'm sure someone took it for kicks, but for the longest time, I thought it was Audrey Musquash. Now...well, maybe, it wasn't Audrey. Have you heard about her father?" Kerry leaned closer. "He was the one doing the break-ins and other creepy stuff. Leah says he's a psycho."

"How does she know?" As far as I knew, none of us really had the full story about what went on with the Musquashes. Once again, I'd underestimated the small town grapevine.

"Leah's aunt is married to Officer MacDonald's wife's cousin. Officer MacDonald told his wife that Jimmy was down making a statement about his dad. Boy, Mr. Musquash had us all fooled." Kerry's eyes sparkled in the sunshine. "Apparently, he was a control freak and wouldn't let his kids have friends or do anything normal. He liked to stalk Audrey...doesn't that give you the creeps?"

I nodded. A shiver travelled up my back as I remembered the feeling of someone watching me.

"I almost feel sorry for her."

I said, "I like Audrey a lot."

We broke apart as footsteps sounded behind us. I turned and saw Jimmy and Audrey watching us with Marilyn and Doris holding hands next to Jimmy.

Marilyn and Doris looked sweet in matching green sundresses and sandals. Their black hair was tied in pigtails, and their smiles were shy. I said to them, "There are pails and shovels over there if you want to go with Leslie and Freddie down that way. I think they're collecting tadpoles, or uh, worms." I avoided Kerry's eyes and pointed to the spot where I could see the tops of Freddie's and Leslie's heads. Marilyn and Doris looked at Jimmy with questioning eyes.

Jimmy said, "Come on. We'll go meet Freddie and Leslie." He picked up the pails and shovels and led them down to the shore.

Kerry and I watched Jimmy walking away from us. I knew she was thinking how good-looking he was, because I was thinking pretty much the same thing. I pulled my eyes away.

"Sit, Audrey." I patted the chair beside me. "You know Kerry from across the lake."

"Hi, Audrey," said Kerry.

Audrey lifted her hand in a salute. She looked at me. "Hey, city girl. I knew you'd be the party type."

"That's me. A party animal. Couldn't your mom make it?"

"No, just small steps. She sent some molasses cookies and a chocolate cake, though. We left it

125

with your grandma in the cottage."

Kerry was strangely silent as Audrey and I talked. I realized we'd become pretty good friends, and I could see Kerry's surprise. After a while, she said to Audrey, "Since I'm president of the student council this year, I'm planning the opening school dance with Mandy Morgan and Leah Pinkett. I wonder if you'd like to help with decorating the school gym this week. Our theme is the seventies—you know, Donna Summers, Bee Gees, John Travolta—disco fever, shake your booty stuff."

Audrey looked at Kerry with an odd grin on her face. I knew as well as Audrey did that she'd been shut out of the school cliques. I wondered how Audrey would respond to Kerry's invitation. Finally, she said, "Sure, Kerry. I can probably help you out."

If Kerry was expecting Audrey to do cartwheels, she was disappointed. Kerry looked unsure of Audrey's sincerity, but said chirpily, "Great. I'll see you around at school and let you know when." She turned to me. "Are you going to be here too in the fall? You could help out with the decorations too, if you are."

"I'm still deciding. I'm leaning that way though."

Kerry and Audrey both said, "Good" at the same time. Then Kerry giggled. "I bet Freddie a month of doing dishes that you'd stay. Looks like I'm going to win."

Audrey looked at me, and her eyes looked sad. She said, "I wouldn't be counting my clean plates yet. It's hard to leave your family, even for a little time, right, city girl?"

I said, "It's a lot to think about, that's for sure."

Kerry flipped her hair back and laughed. "I'd leave my family in a minute. Spread my wings and fly like an eagle."

Audrey said, "Yeah, well. That's the difference between you and Jennifer. She's not flying to somewhere. She's just running away."

I met Audrey's fathomless black eyes. She grinned at me before turning back to listen to Kerry talk about leaving Hawk's Creek to work on a cruise ship as a hostess.

*   *   *

We waited until Joe and Blue came before we ate. Joe brought Grandma a bouquet of wild flowers and a bottle of homemade wine. Dad barbecued chicken, hamburgers and corn, which we ate slathered with butter and salt. There was praise for the potato salad Leslie and I had made, but the best compliments went to Grandma's cherry pies and Mrs. Musquash's chocolate cake. We all patted our tummies and groaned after the last piece of pie had been devoured. Later, Jimmy, Dad and I played a game of horseshoes, and Audrey and Kerry took the other kids for a swim. Mr. and Mrs. Randall, Grandma and Joe sat on the dock talking. Their voices and laughter carried across to the horseshoe pit. Blue lay at Joe's feet with his big head resting on his paws. He'd eaten a piece of chicken and a steak bone that Grandma'd saved for him.

Dad and Jimmy seemed easy with each other. Dad said, "Jimmy, what do you plan to do now with your father gone?"

Mr. Musquash'd been ordered to stay away from Hawk's Creek and his family and would be going to court in a few weeks' time.

Jimmy's horseshoe clinked against the post and rolled away. He said, "The town's offered me Dad's janitor job. I can swing some hours cooking in the evenings too. That ought to keep us afloat."

Dad said, "I'd like to pay you a bit every month to come and do the things that need doing around here. You know, take in the dock, clean up the yard, get the wood in for winter."

Jimmy said, "Between me and Audrey, we'll look after the place. You don't need to pay."

Dad's horseshoe landed square around the post. He smiled and raised his hands in victory. "I wouldn't think of not paying. This is a business deal, Jimmy."

Jimmy looked at Dad and said quietly, "Thanks, Mr. Bannon."

"I'm the one who should thank you, Jimmy. I'm paying for my own peace of mind." He shook Jimmy's hand. "Things have a way of working out for the best. You know that saying, it's always darkest before the dawn?" Dad looked at me and smiled.

I smiled back. "I'll start polishing my sunglasses."

Fifteen

After our guests had left and we'd finished cleaning up, Grandma, Dad, Leslie and I plopped down into chairs in the living room. Leslie crawled into Dad's lap and snuggled into his shoulder.

He asked, "Are you tired, little one?" He rumpled her hair.

She nodded and yawned. "I like Freddie, Doris and Marilyn. Can I come stay next summer too, Grandma?"

Grandma said, "Of course. You girls are welcome any time. Now, why don't you get into your pajamas, dear, and I'll read you a bedtime story?"

Leslie slid from Dad's lap. "Okay, Grandma. You could read me some of *A Wrinkle in Time*. I'm on the third chapter."

"Grandma stood up and reached for Leslie's hand. "Only if you tell me what's happened so far."

Leslie danced from the room, saying, "Once upon a time..."

Dad and I listened to the up and down cadence of Leslie's voice and Grandma's answering murmur. I watched Dad without him seeing me. He had dark hair that was greying at the temples and just enough of a stubble on his face to make him look rugged. I remember Ambie saying that my mother was crazy not to give him another chance. Ambie said that he'd be snapped up in no time. That thought didn't make me too happy.

Dad looked at me and said, "How about we go down to the dock and listen for the loon?"

"Okay." I jumped up and grabbed my jacket with my good hand. The evenings had started to cool off once the sun went down. We got a couple of flashlights from the kitchen, and Dad took a beer from the fridge.

We made our way down the path to the water. Dad took two of the lawn chairs and set them on the dock. We sat side by side and listened to the night sounds, as I had done so many evenings with Audrey.

"Look," Dad said, pointing towards the middle of the lake. "Isn't that the loon?" Moonlight sparkled across the water and I could just make out a dark shadow bobbing up and down near the big rock.

"Yes, but he's not calling tonight."

"Give him time."

I said, "Isn't it great here at the lake with Grandma? It's so restful."

"I'm glad you've had this time to think about things, Jen. You know, Leslie and I are leaving tomorrow."

The suddenness of their departure felt like a weight in my stomach. "So soon?"

"Yeah, I have to get her set for school next week. Listen," Dad said. "Isn't it magical?" We listened to the loon's haunting call like a crescendo across the lake.

"Do you think he's calling for his mate? Grandma says they mate for life." I thought about Mom and Dad, and Mom and Mr. Putterman.

"Life is simpler in the animal kingdom sometimes, isn't it, Jenny bear?" he said as if he'd read my mind.

I said angrily, "Why can't you and Mom get back together? Why does she have to break our family apart?"

Dad said slowly, "It's not your mother's fault, and you mustn't blame her. We both made mistakes, but I made the biggest one when I left Springhills. I should never have run away from our problems."

"Do you think that's what I'm doing too?" I thought of Audrey's identical observation that afternoon.

"Well, I think so, because I did the same thing. I can tell you though, Jen, it was short-term gain for longtime pain. I wish now I'd faced things when I had the chance."

"I'm so mad at her, it makes me feel sick."

"You should be angry at me too, kiddo. You gotta realize though, laying blame just gets in the way. Your mom loves you and Leslie more than anything. You know, she even asked me if

131

she should call off the wedding if it would bring you home."

"She did?"

"I told her that wasn't something I could decide. She owed it to herself to do what makes her happy."

"Well, I don't want to live with her and Mr. Putterman. I just don't want to."

"Your mom and I thought you might like to live with me. I've got an offer in on a little house near the shop. If you like it, I'll seal the deal."

"Mom wouldn't mind? She never wanted me to be around you much."

Dad laughed. "She's agreed. We had a long talk last week, and she thinks maybe being angry with me wasn't too productive. Your refusal to come home led us both to some soul-searching. In the end, what matters is your happiness and Leslie's happiness."

"I want you and Mom to be happy too."

"We're getting there, but we can't be happy if you and Leslie are miserable."

"Where'll Leslie live?"

"She'll have a bedroom in both houses. I can take her when your mom's working. I guess you know I'd like her to be with us as much as possible. And you can stay at your mom's whenever you like."

Suddenly, I knew what I wanted, and it was to live with Dad and Leslie in Springhills.

I leaned over and wrapped my good arm around Dad's neck and kissed his cheek.

I asked, "Does this little house have a backyard and a pool?"

"It's got room for the biggest wading pool money can buy at Canadian Tire."

"That'll do."

Dad sighed. "Leslie and your mom and I need you, Jen. We love you very much."

"I know, Dad. I love you too."

We sat quietly and listened to the wild calling of the loon. It echoed across the water—a wild song of longing.

Finally, Dad stood up. "Coming?" he asked, stretching and then bending to pick up his lawn chair.

I stood too. "You can have my chair, but is it okay if I stay a few minutes more?"

"Sure. I'll see you back at the cottage." Dad turned and crossed the length of the dock. I listened to his footsteps disappear into the darkness.

I walked to the end of the dock and leaned back to look at the carpet of stars above my head. The moon was nearly full and shone like a golden lantern over the dark outline of the far shore. I breathed in the spruce trees and the lake and the cool end of summer night. The loon called one last time before it fell silent. "I'll be back, Hawk's Creek," I yelled across the lake. "Don't ever change. I'll be back again next summer!"

I took one last look for the loon's shadow on the water before turning towards the lights of the cottage and my family waiting for me inside.

Photo by Fred Taylor

Brenda Chapman grew up in Terrace Bay, Ontario. An avid reader with a love for writing, she studied English at Lakehead University in Thunder Bay and attended teachers' college at Queen's University in Kingston, Ontario. Upon completion, she moved to Ottawa, where she became a special education teacher. Brenda taught reading and language arts to children, teenagers and adults for nearly fifteen years. She currently works as a communications advisor for the Canadian federal government in Ottawa, Ontario. *Hiding in Hawk's Creek* is her second novel for young readers and the sequel to *Running Scared.*